The U.S.S. Excalibur *was under attack. . . .*

Captain's Log, Stardate 50926.1—Captain Mackenzie Calhoun recording. The *Excalibur* has been endeavoring to provide humanitarian aid to the stranded vessel *Cambon* and its four dozen passengers presently in sickbay. However, we now find ourselves face to face with an unexpected intruder, who has opened fire on us.

First Officer's Log, Stardate 50926.1—Commander Elizabeth Shelby recording. Our attempt to effect repairs on a stranded private crew ship, the *Cambon,* populated by refugees from the fallen Thallonian government, has been interrupted by the appearance of an unknown vessel, which is reacting in a hostile manner to what is undoubtedly perceived as our trespass. Ideally, Captain Calhoun should be able to handle this matter in a calm and reasonable manner. . . .

STAR TREK®
NEW FRONTIER

BOOK THREE

THE TWO-FRONT WAR

PETER DAVID

POCKET BOOKS
New York   London   Toronto   Sydney   Tokyo   Singapore

An *Original* Publication of POCKET BOOKS

POCKET BOOKS, a division of Simon & Schuster Inc.
1230 Avenue of the Americas, New York, NY 10020

This book is published by Pocket Books, a division of Simon & Schuster Inc., under exclusive license from Paramount Pictures.

ISBN: 0-671-01397-1

First Pocket Books printing August 1997

10 9 8 7 6 5 4 3 2 1

MACKENZIE

Captain's Log, Stardate 50926.1—The Excalibur *has been endeavoring to provide humanitarian aid to the stranded vessel* Cambon *and its four dozen passengers presently in sickbay. However, we now find ourselves face-to-face with an unexpected intruder, who has opened fire on us.*

First Officer's Log, Stardate 50926.1—Our attempt to effect repairs on a stranded private crew ship, the Cambon, *populated by refugees from the fallen Thallonian government, has been interrupted by the appearance of an unknown vessel, which is reacting in a hostile manner to what is undoubtedly perceived as our trespass. Ideally, Captain Calhoun should be able to handle this matter in a calm and reasonable manner.*

I.

"I want to blow those bastards out of space."

The *Excalibur* had just been rocked by the opening salvo from the black-and-silver ship that hung 100,000 kilometers to starboard. The phase/plasma cannons had pounded against the starship's shields, firing specially created "phaser/plasma" essentially designed not to smash shields apart, but instead to determine the wave harmonics of the shielding and basically eat through them with violent force. The first of the blasts went a long way toward cracking through the primary shields, and the *Excalibur* was jolted by the impact.

Nonetheless, even though the starship had been subjected to this most undignified and unprovoked attack, Captain Calhoun's angry order prompted a startled gasp from Commander Shelby. "Captain—!"

"Save the indignation, Commander. I didn't say I *would* . . . merely that I wanted to. Still, the day's young," and Calhoun rose from his chair, looking energized and confident. "Lefler, damage report."

"Some damage on primary shields," Robin Lefler reported from ops. "No structural damage. Forward shields at eighty percent and holding."

"McHenry . . ." began Calhoun.

And to his surprise, the normally laid-back helmsman said in staccato fashion, "I've angled the ship to protect the damaged shields, sir. Taking evasive action." He caught Lefler's look from the corner of his eye and turned to glance at the captain. "Was that jumping the gun, sir?"

"Yes, but I'll let it go this time," replied Calhoun, who had in fact been about to issue exactly those orders. "Mr. Boyajian, have you raised them yet?"

"Not yet, sir." Boyajian, a tall, black-haired tactical specialist, had stepped in to cover for Zak Kebron while the security chief was off-ship.

Calhoun spoke briskly and forcefully, yet in a manner so unhurried that it gave the impression he felt fairly unthreatened by the present situation. Whether that was truly the case or not was impossible to tell. "Keep trying, but meantime see if you can determine where their key points of vulnerability are and target them."

"Trying, Captain. Tough to scan them through their shields."

"Do your best." He turned toward the science station. "Lieutenant Soleta, any thoughts on the ship's pedigree?"

"Although the vessel bears passing similarities with Kreel vessels, it is not of that race," she said as she checked her scanners. "It will take time to make a full analysis."

"Fine, you've got twenty seconds."

"I appreciate the leisure time, sir."

"They're coming around again," warned Shelby.

"Firing again!" Boyajian warned.

Two phase/plasma bolts streaked out from the underside of the black-and-silver ship. Mark McHenry's eyes seemed to glitter with an almost demented glee as his fingers flew over the controls with such speed that Lefler, sitting not ten feet away, couldn't even see them.

The twin blasts arced right for the front of the saucer section, and would have struck it cleanly had not the *Excalibur* suddenly—with alacrity and grace—executed a forty-five-degree roll on her horizontal axis. Terms such as "sideways" had no meaning in the depth of space when there was no other body, such as a planet, to relate it to. Nonetheless, "sideways" was what the *Excalibur* suddenly was as the plasma blasts shot past her, bracketing her on either side.

"Excellent!" Shelby called out. McHenry had had no more vocal critic or detractor than Shelby when she had first seen him at his post, apparently unfocused and uninterested. But faced with a crisis,

McHenry had reacted with ingenuity and full capability.

McHenry's response to Shelby's spontaneous praise was to turn and grin at her.

Soleta, who appeared oblivious to McHenry's maneuvering, glanced up from her science station. "Sir, I believe that bulge to their aft section is the key to their propulsion system . . . some sort of a concentrated ion glide."

"Mr. Boyajian, target it, ready phasers for a three-second shot at full strength. Then put me on ship-to-ship."

"Aye, sir, but I can't promise they're listening."

"I'll take that chance. Oh, and the moment I get to five, fire."

"You're on intership, Captain," said Boyajian, "but what did you mean by—?"

Calhoun didn't give him the opportunity to finish the question. Instead, in a no-nonsense tone, he said, "Attention alien vessel. This is Captain Calhoun of the Federation starship *Excalibur*. Your attack is unprovoked. We will give you to the count of five to back off, or we will open fire."

Understanding the earlier order, Boyajian's finger hovered over the firing control.

And Calhoun, without hesitation, said, "One . . . two . . . *five.*"

Boyajian fired the phaser reflexively upon hearing the command, acting so automatically that the phasers had already been unleashed before he realized that a few numbers had been missing in the countdown.

The phasers lashed out, striking the attacking vessel directly in the section that Soleta had suggested. The attacker rocked wildly, the phasers coruscating off the shields.

"Direct hit," Boyajian reported. "Their shields held, but I don't think they were particularly thrilled."

"I didn't expect to damage them," said Calhoun. "Not with a three-second burst."

"A warning shot," Shelby realized. "To let them know that we've targeted a vulnerable area."

Calhoun nodded, and that was when Boyajian said, "We're getting an incoming hail, sir."

"Good. Let them sweat a few moments before putting them on."

In a low voice so as not to sound openly questioning of her superior officer in front of the rest of the bridge crew, Shelby murmured, "If you wanted to warn them, you could have fired at half-strength. Perhaps even fired across their path rather than an invasive direct strike."

"If I have a bow and arrow, Commander, I don't shoot a padded shaft to my target's left in order to express my annoyance. I fire a steel-tipped arrow into his leg. That's my idea of a warning shot."

"You're the Gandhi of the spaceways, Captain."

He smiled and then said, "Put me on with them, Boyajian."

"You're on, sir."

"This is Captain Calhoun of the *Excalibur*," he said. "Identify yourselves and prepare to stand down from hostilities. Otherwise I can assure you that you will not leave this confrontation in one piece."

The screen shimmered for a moment, and the commander (presumably) of the opposing vessel appeared.

Although distinguishing gender was frequently a bit problematic in any first encounter, the *Excalibur*'s opponent looked distinctly female. Moreover, by Earth standards she appeared almost angelic. She was hairless, her skin golden, her brow slightly distended in a manner that was—amazingly enough—still attractive. It was difficult to make out the color of her eyes, but when she tilted her head they seemed to glow with an almost purple sheen. When she spoke, her voice had a vibrato to it that gave it a somewhat musical quality.

"I am Laheera of Nelkar," she replied. "Do you wish to discuss terms of your surrender?"

"Surrender?" Calhoun cast a skeptical glance at Shelby as if to say, *Do you hear this?* He looked back to Laheera. "You expect me—a Starfleet captain—to surrender my vessel on our maiden voyage to the first opponent who looks to pose a challenge? Sorry. That's not my style."

"And is your style trespass, then? We know your type, Calhoun," said Laheera. Her voice was such that, even when annoyed, she had a tone of amusement to her. "Our once-orderly sector is now subject to the attentions of scavengers and pirates. People who will take every opportunity to ravage us, to feed on helplessness. We must protect ourselves."

"I can appreciate that," replied Calhoun, "but you've misjudged us. We're here only to help."

"How do we know? Why, there is a transport vessel right next to you that is empty and damaged. How do we know you haven't picked it clean of whatever it might have had to offer?"

"The transport vessel's crew is aboard this ship. We were lending humanitarian aid. If you wish, I can have you speak to its captain and a delegation of its crew."

Laheera glanced to the side of the screen and murmured something, as if consulting with someone unseen. Then she looked back and said, "That would be acceptable."

"Give us five minutes. Calhoun out." He didn't even wait for the screen to blink off as he said, "Bridge to sickbay."

"Sickbay, Dr. Selar here," came the crisp response.

"Doctor, I'd like you to get Captain Hufmin and a couple of representatives of the *Cambon* passengers up here immediately. Whoever is healthiest and is qualified to speak on their behalf. And make it fast."

"Will three minutes suffice?"

"Make it two. Calhoun out." He promptly turned to Boyajian and said, "Can you raise the *Marquand?*"

"Aye, sir."

"Good. Get me Si Cwan on subspace. I want to see what he knows about these 'Nelkar' people."

He looked to Shelby and he knew what she was thinking. She was musing that if Calhoun hadn't let Si Cwan and Zak Kebron head out in the runabout for the purpose of rendezvous with the ship *Kayven Ryin,* then he would be aboard the *Excalibur* now, in a position to be of some use. Shelby, however, was far too good an officer to voice those thoughts . . . at least, while other crewmen were around. So instead she nodded noncommittally and simply said, "Good plan, sir."

"Zoran, it's slowing down!"

Aboard the *Kayven Ryin,* a group of Thallonians had been watching the approach of the *Marquand* with tremendous interest and smug excitement. For what seemed the hundredth time, Zoran had checked over his disruptor, making certain that the energy cartridge was fully charged. But with the alarmed shout from one of his associates, Rojam, Zoran tore himself away from his preoccupation with his weapon.

Rojam was correct. The *Marquand,* dispatched by the *Excalibur* and bearing the unknowing target of Zoran's interest—named Lord Si Cwan, former prince of the Thallonian Empire—had been proceeding at a brisk pace toward the *Kayven Ryin.*

"They suspect," muttered Rojam.

"Do something, then," snapped Zoran. "We can't

be this close to having Si Cwan in our hands, only to let him slip through our fingers now! I must have his throat in my hands, so that I can squeeze the life from him myself!" The other Thallonians nodded in agreement, which was hardly surprising. Whenever Zoran spoke, the others had a tendency to concur.

Reactivating the comm channel, Rojam hailed the oncoming runabout. He tried not to sound nervous, apprehensive, or all that eager, although a little of any of that would have been understandable. After all, they were representing themselves as frightened, stranded passengers aboard a crippled science vessel. A degree of nervousness under the circumstances would be right in line with the scenario they were presenting. "Shuttle craft *Marquand,* is there a problem? You seem to be slowing." He paused and then added, "Aren't you going to help us?"

There was no reply at first and another of the Thallonians, a shorter and more aggressive man named Juif, whispered, "Target them! Target them! Use exterior weapons and blast them into atoms! Hurry, before it's too late!"

"They're at the outer edge of the firing range," Zoran noted angrily. "We likely couldn't do them any significant damage, and they'd still be in a position to get away. Hell, their instruments would probably inform them we're locking on to them. They'd leap into warp space and be gone before we got a shot off." The edge to his voice became more pronounced as he said in a threatening manner, "Rojam . . ."

"They're not responding."

"That is unacceptable. Get them on the line."

"But if they won't respon—"

Zoran's large hand clamped down on the back of Rojam's neck, and the latter felt as if his head was about to be torn from his shoulders. "Providence has delivered Si Cwan to us," snarled Zoran, "and I will not have him escape. Now get them on the line!"

Never had Rojam been more convinced that his demise was imminent. And then, as if in answer to unvoiced prayers, a gravelly voice came over the speaker. "This is Lieutenant Kebron of the *Marquand*. Sit tight, *Kayven Ryin*. We're just dealing with a communiqué from our main vessel. Kebron out."

"Raise them again!" urged Zoran.

"I can't. The channel's gone dead."

"If they get away," Zoran said meaningfully, "that channel won't be the only thing around here that's dead."

Si Cwan stroked his chin thoughtfully. "The Nelkarites, eh?"

"You know them?" Calhoun's voice came over the subspace radio. "Are they trustworthy?"

"Nowadays, there are few in Sector 221-G whom I would consider absolutely trustworthy," Si Cwan told him. "Relatively speaking, the Nelkar had been fairly harmless. Never started any wars, more than happy to accept Thallonian rule. However . . ."

"However?" prompted Calhoun when the word seemed simply to dangle there.

"Well . . . they're a scavenger race, by and large. Fairly limited in their design and potential. They tend to cobble their vessels together from whatever they can find, using technology that they don't always understand."

Soleta's voice was audible over the link as she commented, "That would explain the somewhat haphazard design of their vessel."

"Does that answer your questions, Captain?" asked Si Cwan, not quite able to keep the urgency out of his voice. "Because if it's all the same to you—"

"Stay on station. Do not proceed to the *Kayven Ryin* until you hear back from us."

"But Captain—!"

"I want to get matters sorted out on this end before you board that vessel, and I want to know I can get in touch with you. If the comm system on the *Kayven Ryin* goes out, you'll be incommunicado."

"Captain—!" Si Cwan tried to protest.

But Calhoun wouldn't hear any of it. Instead he said preemptively, "Did you copy those orders, Lieutenant Kebron?"

Without hesitation, Kebron said, "Understood, Captain."

"Excalibur out."

Making no attempt to cover his anger, Si Cwan sprang to his feet and slammed his fists into the ceiling of the shuttle craft. Kebron watched him impassively. "What do you think you're doing?"

"I'm getting angry!" snapped Si Cwan. He began to pace the interior of the shuttle craft like a tiger. "Why, don't you ever get angry?"

"I try not to," said Kebron evenly. "If I lose control, things tend to get broken."

"Things. What kinds of things," demanded Si Cwan without much interest.

"Oh . . . heads . . . backs . . . necks . . ."

Captain Hufmin of the damaged vessel *Cambon,* along with two of the refugees—a husband and wife named Boretskee and Cary, who had developed into a kind of leaders-by-default—sat in the conference lounge with Calhoun and Shelby. On the screen was Laheera of Nelkar, and it was quite apparent to Calhoun that Hufmin and company were spellbound by her.

"You understand that we were only concerned about the welfare of your passengers," Laheera said to Calhoun in that wonderfully musical voice of hers. "Let us not lose sight of one simple truth: This is our sector of space. You are merely a visitor here. It is to our interest to watch out for one another. It is difficult to know whom to trust."

"Understood," Calhoun said neutrally.

"Captain Hufmin . . . I extend to you and your . . . *cargo,"* she seemed amused by the notion, "sanctuary on Nelkar. We welcome you with open arms."

Boretskee and Cary looked at each other with undisguised joy and relief. "We accept your offer," they said.

"Excellent. I shall inform my homeworld." The screen shimmered and she was gone.

"Now, wait a minute," said Shelby. "Are you quite certain about this?"

"Commander, we are not pioneers," Cary replied. "We are not intrepid adventurers like yourselves. We're just trying to survive, that's all. Whether we survive on their world or somewhere outside of the Thallonian Empire, what difference does it make?"

"Isn't there an old Earth saying about any port in a storm?" Hufmin reminded them.

"Yes, and there's also one about fools rushing in," said Calhoun.

Boretskee bristled a bit. "I can't say I appreciate being considered a 'fool,' Captain."

"I didn't say that—"

Cary cut in. "We are grateful to you for all you've done for us. You saved our lives. For that our next generation of children will be named for you. But, Captain," and Cary gestured as if trying to encompass the whole of the galaxy, "this environment you sail through—space—you're comfortable in it. You've made your peace with it. But myself, Boretskee, the others in our group . . . we're not space-faring types. This vacuum . . . it presses on us. Intimidates us. We almost died in it. If the Nelkarites offer us safe escort and a life on their world, we'll happily embrace it."

Hufmin took in both Shelby and Calhoun with a bland shrug. "Look . . . I'm just a hired gun here. They're the passengers. Barring desires that run contrary to the safety of my vessel, I'm obligated to take them where they want to go."

"Perhaps. But I'm not," Calhoun said.

They looked at him, a bit appalled. "Captain . . . you wouldn't," said Boretskee.

"I have to do what I think is right. And I'm loath to thrust you into a potentially dangerous situation . . ."

"We're already in a potentially dangerous situation," Cary pointed out. "We're in the depths of space. That's dangerous enough as far as we're concerned. It almost killed us once. We have no desire to give it a second opportunity."

"With all respect, Captain, this shouldn't be your decision," Boretskee said.

"With all respect, sir . . . that is precisely what it is," replied Calhoun. He rose from his seat and turned away from them, his hands draped behind his back. "I'll let you know what I decide presently. That will be all."

"Now wait one minute—"

"I believe, sir, that the captain said that would be all," Shelby said calmly, her fingers interlaced on the table in front of her. "Temporary quarters have been set up to house you and your fellow passengers. Perhaps the time could be well spent discussing your options with them . . . just in the event that you're not all of the same mind."

"Apparently what we decide is irrelevant," said Boretskee challengingly. His fists were tightly clenched; it was clear that he was a bit of a scrapper, just waiting for Calhoun to react in some aggressive manner. When Calhoun did not even turn, however, Boretskee continued angrily, "Wouldn't you say so, Captain?"

Calhoun turned to look at him, and his purple eyes were as sympathetic as a black hole. "Yes. I would." The air turned more frigid with each word.

To his credit, Boretskee didn't seem inclined to back down. But Cary headed off any continuing hostility as she tugged on Boretskee's arm and he allowed himself to be led out of the room. Captain Hufmin paused at the door long enough to say, "Look, Captain . . . I don't give a damn either way. I'm making almost no money on this job as it is. But for what it's worth, these are people who have lost everything. Be a shame if they lost their self-respect, too."

Shelby waited until the moment that Hufmin was gone and out of earshot, and then she said to Calhoun, "It's not your choice, you know."

He raised an eyebrow. "Pardon?"

"Regs are clear on this. These people know where they want to go. You don't have any conceivable grounds upon which to overrule their desire."

"Yes, I do."

"That being?"

"My gut."

She leaned back, arms folded. "Your gut," she

said, unenthused. "Funny. I don't remember reading about that in my Intro to Regs class back at the Academy. Guts, I mean."

"Nelkar smells wrong."

"First your stomach, now your nose. Are you a Starfleet captain or a gourmet?"

And to her utter surprise, he slammed the conference table with an iron fist. The noise startled her and she jumped slightly, but quickly composed herself. And just as quickly as she reined herself in, so did Calhoun. "I'm dealing with subtleties, Commander. Regulations aren't created for subtleties. They're created as sweeping generalizations to handle all situations. But not every situation."

"And it can't be that every situation, you do whatever the hell you want. Nor can it be that you let your frustration get to you so quickly and so easily."

"I'm not frustrated," Calhoun said. "I simply know what I know. And what I know is that Nelkar seems off. I don't trust Laheera."

"Be that as it may, Mac . . . do you want to be a dictator? With your history, do you feel comfortable with that label?"

He smiled thinly. "You always know just what to say."

"Long practice." She sauntered toward him, stopping several feet away. "Look, Mac . . . for what it's worth, I respect your gut, your nose . . . all your instincts. But that has to be balanced against conducting ourselves in an orderly fashion. We're the only Starfleet vessel out here. We're here at a time of disarray. We have to stand for something, and we can't simply come in and throw our weight around. It's patronizing; don't you see that?"

"Yes, I see that. By the same token, should I deliberately allow people to go into a dangerous situation when I can prevent them from doing so?"

She was silent for a long moment. "You mean like with the captain of the *Grissom?*"

With a deep sigh, Calhoun told her, "Eppy . . . you know I admire you. Respect you. Still have deep feelings for you, as much as I hate to admit it . . . although certainly not romantic, God knows . . ."

"Of course not," she quickly agreed.

"But so help me, if you bring up the *Grissom* again, I may become violent."

"Really. Try it and I'll kick your ass. Sir."

And he laughed. "You know . . . I'll bet you could, at that." But then he became serious again. "Very well, Commander. But this will be done on my terms."

"Your terms being . . . ?"

For reply, he tapped his comm unit. "Bridge . . . open a hailing frequency to the Nelkar ship. Pipe it down here."

Within moments Laheera was smiling at them in that beatific manner she had. "Greetings," she said. "Are you preparing to transport your charges over to our ship?"

"Actually," replied Calhoun, "I was anticipating that we would transport them ourselves, if it is all the same to you."

Shelby looked from Calhoun to Laheera, trying to get some hint of her state of mind. But if Laheera seemed at all disconcerted by Calhoun's statement, she did not give the slightest sign. "That would be perfectly acceptable. I will send you the coordinates for our homeworld. Laheera out."

When she blinked out, Shelby asked, "What about the *Cambon?* We can't haul it along at warp speed."

"We'll cut her loose and leave her here to drift until we come back for her," he said after a moment's thought. "Considering the condition she's in, I hardly think we have to worry about scavengers."

"Bridge to Captain Calhoun," came McHenry's voice.

"Calhoun here."

"Captain, we've gotten coordinates for Nelkar." He paused. "Were we expecting them?"

"Yes, we were. Warp five would get us there when, Mr. McHenry?"

"At warp five? Two hours, ten minutes, sir. They're not all that far."

Shelby commented, "Considering their own vessel isn't exactly the most advanced I've seen, I can't say I'm surprised. That still leaves us with one outstanding problem."

"Yes, I'm quite aware of that. McHenry, set course for Nelkar, warp five. Then have Mr. Boyajian patch me through to the *Marquand.* Let's make sure we're not leaving them in the lurch."

"You're making the right decision, sir," said Shelby.

"I'm so relieved that you approve, Commander." He grimaced. "My only problem is . . . you know that unpleasant feeling I've got about the Nelkarites?"

"Yes?"

"Well . . . now I'm starting to get it about the *Marquand* and its rendezvous with the *Kayven Ryin*. I hope that wasn't a mistake as well."

"Captain, if you keep second-guessing your judgments, you're going to make yourself insane."

"Why, Commander . . . I thought you decided I was insane the day I broke off our engagement."

And with a contemptuous chuckle, she said, "Captain . . . I hate to inform you . . . but I broke it off. Not you." She strode out of the conference lounge, leaving an amused Calhoun shaking his head. But then the amusement slowly evaporated as the reality set in.

He didn't like the situation. Not at all.

For years he had basically been his own boss. He had answered to no one except, in a very distant manner, Admiral Nechayev. He had been bound by no rules except those of common sense, and made decisions that were answerable only to himself. It had been an extremely free manner in which to operate.

But now . . . now he had rules hanging over him whichever way he turned. He had operated under rules before, yes . . . but he had been the one making the rules. Back when he'd been a freedom fighter on his native Xenex, his wiles and craftiness had earned him the respect of those around him and they obeyed him. They obeyed him unthinkingly, unhesitatingly. Had he told them to throw themselves on their swords, they would have done so with the firm conviction that there was a damned good reason for it.

But that wasn't the case here. Yes, he was captain. Yes, he was obeyed. But that obedience came as a result of a long tradition and history that dictated that obedience. They answered to the rank, not to him. When it came to he himself, he could sense that there were still double-takes or second thoughts. His crew—Shelby in particular—gave thought to his orders, questioned him, challenged him. It irked him, angered him.

And yet . . . and yet . . .

Shouldn't that really please him? Shouldn't that be something that made him happy rather than disconcerted him? After all, he had lived in an environment where blind obedience was expected as a matter of course, and punished if not given. The Xenexians had lived under the thumb of the Danterians, and during that time the Danterians had not been exactly reluctant to show who was boss at any given moment. They had unhesitatingly used the Xenexians as their objects, their toys, their playthings to dispose of at a whim or exploit as they saw fit. Young M'k'n'zy of Calhoun had seen those activities and a cold fury had built within him. Built and built until it had exploded into rebellion, and through sheer force of will he had brought an entire race with him.

Yes, he had indeed seen firsthand the dangers of requiring unquestioned obedience. At the same time, he was frustrated that the same rules under which he oftentimes felt constricted were what guaranteed that his own people would do what he told them to. He wanted more than that.

Time, a voice in his head consoled him. These things required time. He had always been impatient, always wanted everything at whatever moment he wanted it. It was an attitude that had, in the past, stood him in good stead. When tribal elders had told him that someday, someday in the far future, the Xenexians would be free, young M'k'n'zy had not settled for that. "Someday" was too ephemeral, too useless a concept for him. He wanted "someday" to be right then and there. He would make his own "somedays."

He smiled at the absurdity of it all. Despite everything he'd gone through, everything he'd seen, there was still an impatient young Xenexian within him who did not understand the need for patience. A young Xenexian who wanted everything immediately, and who had no use whatsoever for "someday."

He tapped his comm badge. "Calhoun to Shelby."

"Shelby here," came the prompt reply.

"Have we been in communication with Kebron and Si Cwan?"

"Yes, sir. They, in turn, have spoken with the crew of the *Kayven Ryin*. Although they are in distress, there is no immediate danger to them. They report life-support systems are still on line. Kebron and Cwan intended to board the *Kayven Ryin* and lend whatever aid they can until we rendezvous with them."

"Very well. Best speed to Nelkar, then . . . on my order," he added as an afterthought.

"On your order, sir," she said. Then there was a pause. "Captain . . ."

"Yes, Commander?"

"We're waiting on your order."

He smiled to the empty room. "Yes. I know." He paused a moment longer, then said simply, "Now."

"Now it is, sir."

It was a small pleasure, making them wait in anticipation of the order. Childish, perhaps. A juvenile reminder of who was in charge, but he found that it gave him amusement. And lately he'd had very little of that.

"Oh, and Commander," he said as an afterthought.

"Yes, sir."

"Just for your information: *I* broke it off. Calhoun out."

* * *

On the bridge of the *Excalibur,* Lefler turned in her seat and looked quizzically at Shelby. She noted that it seemed as if Shelby's chest were shaking in amusement. "He 'broke it off,' Commander?"

"So he claims, Lieutenant," replied Shelby.

From the science station, Soleta inquired, "Will he be needing someone to reattach it?"

And then she stared at Shelby in confusion as Shelby, unable to contain it anymore, laughed out loud.

SI CWAN

II.

ZORAN THOUGHT THAT HE was going to go out of his mind.

He felt as if the damned shuttle craft had been hanging there forever, tantalizingly, frustratingly just out of reach. He had wanted to send multiple messages to it, telling them to get over to the ship immediately, that help was desperately needed, that they were going to die within seconds if immediate aid were not provided. But Rojam had cautioned against it. "They have their own instrumentation," he advised Zoran. "If we try to trick them, if we tell them there's immediate danger when there isn't, they'll be able to see through it."

"Maybe we should take that chance," Zoran urged.

"Then again, maybe we should not," fired back

Rojam. "What should we say? That our engines are in danger of exploding? That our life-support systems are failing? These are not possibilities, because their own onboard readings will tell them that we're lying. And if they know that we're lying, then they're going to start to wonder what the truth is. And if they do that, then we have a major problem."

"Damn them!" snarled Zoran, pacing the room. His long and powerful legs carried him quickly around the perimeter, and his blue body armor clacked as he moved. His red face was darker than usual as he mused on the frustration facing him. "Si Cwan wasn't part of the plan, but now that he's here . . . damn him and damn them all!"

"Damning them isn't going to do a bit of g—" Rojam began to say. But then he stopped as a blinking light on the control panel caught his attention. "Incoming hail from the *Marquand,*" he said.

"It's about time!" Zoran fairly shouted.

"Will you calm down?" Juif said in exasperation. "If we're in communication with them and Si Cwan hears your bellowing, that's going to be the end of that!"

With effort, Zoran brought himself under control as Rojam answered the hail. "We were beginning to wonder, *Marquand.*"

"We needed to speak with the *Excalibur,*" came the deep voice that they knew to be the passenger other than Si Cwan. "What is your present emergency status? How long can you survive aboard your vessel?"

Zoran was gesturing that Rojam should lie, but Rojam was quite certain that that was not the way to go. He believed in all the reasons that he'd put forward to Zoran, and there was one other element as well: If Si Cwan was aboard the *Marquand,* not all the hosts of hell would get him to depart without his sister at his side.

"Lie!" Zoran hissed in a very low voice. "They're going to *leave* if we don't!" And the way his fist was clenching and unclenching told Rojam a very disturbing truth: namely, that if answered the question from the *Marquand* accurately and then the shuttle craft turned and left for the mother ship, Rojam would very likely not live out the hour. Not given the mood that Zoran was presently in.

But he felt he had to trust his instincts, and on that basis, he said, "Life-support systems are presently holding together. Our main problem is in engineering; our propulsion systems are out. Our batteries are running down and we likely could not survive indefinitely, but for the very immediate future, the danger level is tolerable."

There was a silence that seemed infinitely long, and Rojam could practically hear his life span shortening. But then the voice said, "This is the *Marquand.* With your permission, we will come aboard and give what aid we can, while we wait for the *Excalibur* to rendezvous with us. Will that be acceptable?"

"Yes. Absolutely acceptable," said Rojam, relief

flooding through him. Behind him he could sense Zoran nodding in approval.

"Just one thing . . . ?"

"Yes, *Marquand?*"

"Please put the passenger called Kalinda on with us. Her brother would like to speak with her."

"Uhm . . ." Suddenly sweat began to beat on Rojam's crimson forehead, his grimacing white teeth standing out in stark relief to his face. "Just a moment, please." He switched off the comm channel and then turned to Zoran. "Now what?"

"Now?" Zoran smiled. "Now . . . we give them what they asked for."

Si Cwan stared in confusion at Zak Kebron. "Why did you ask them to put Kalinda on?"

"Because," Kebron said slowly and deliberately— which was more or less how he said everything—"I am being cautious. It's my job to watch out for everyone on board the *Excalibur*. That even includes those who have no business being there at all."

"I appreciate the thought."

"Don't. As noted: It's my job." He paused. "Would you know your sister's voice if you heard it?"

"Of course." He waited for a response, but none seemed to be immediately in evidence. Concern began to grow within him. "You don't think there's a problem."

"I always think there's a problem," replied

Kebron. "It saves time. And lives." He checked his instruments. "Their life-support appears stable. Pity. If they had lied about that, I would have known that there was something wrong. Perhaps it is a more subtle trap."

"Or perhaps they're truly in distress. But then . . . why hasn't Kalinda come on—?" It was a disturbing thought. He had simply taken for granted that his sister was truly a passenger on the science vessel. The notion that she might not be was agonizing for him. To have his hopes raised and then dashed in such a manner . . .

But even more disturbing, he realized, was the concept that he had not questioned it for one moment. One did not acquire or maintain power by being easily duped. Had he let his love for his sister, his desire to try and reconstruct some semblance of his former life, completely blind him to all caution? That was a very, very dangerous mind-set to have.

And then a girlish voice came over the comm system. "Si Cwan?" it said.

Si Cwan came close to knocking Kebron aside— or as close as one can come to budging someone who is essentially a walking mountain of granite. "Kally?" he practically shouted.

"Si Cwan, is that you?"

"Yes . . . yes it is . . . Kally, everything is going to be all right . . ."

"I'm so glad to hear your voice, Si Cwan . . ."

Si Cwan felt himself choking with relief, but then Kebron said in a sharp whisper, "Ask her something only she would know."

"What?" He seemed to have trouble focusing, which of course bugged the hell out of Kebron.

"Something only she would know," he repeated.

Slowly, Si Cwan nodded. "Kally . . . remember that time? That time shortly before we had to leave? Remember that? When I said that I would always be there for you? Remember, when we spoke at our special place?"

There was a short hesitation, one that made Si Cwan wonder ever so briefly, and then her voice said, "You mean that time by the Fire Falls? That?"

He closed his eyes and nodded. Kalinda, meanwhile, naturally couldn't see him as she continued, "Si Cwan? Is that what you're talking about?"

"Yes, that's it."

"Why did you want to know about that?"

"Just being careful. You understand. These days, we can't be too careful." He looked triumphantly at Kebron, who merely grunted and edged the ship forward toward the *Kayven Ryin*.

"Okay, Si Cwan . . . whatever you say."

"We'll be there in a few minutes, Kally. Don't worry. We'll be right along."

"Okay, Si Cwan. I'll see you soon." And the connection broke off.

And the moment that happened, Kebron brought the ship to a dead halt in space. Si Cwan was immediately aware of it. "What are you doing?" he demanded.

Zak Kebron turned in his chair. "I don't like it."

"What?"

"I said I don't like it."

Si Cwan appeared ready to explode. His body was trembling with repressed fury. "Now, you listen to me," he said sharply. "I know what this is about."

"Do you," asked Kebron, unimpressed by Si Cwan's ire.

"It's not enough that you continue to resent me, or deny my right to be aboard the *Excalibur*. But now . . . now you'd hurt a young girl whom you've never met . . . who's never done anything to you . . ."

"It must be nice to be a prince," Kebron said evenly, "and know everything there is to know about everything." Then he glanced at the control board. "They're hailing us."

"Of course they are! They're wondering what's happening." Si Cwan came around his seat and confronted Kebron, fury building. "They have no idea that a resentful Brikar is endeavoring to make my life impossible!"

Kebron ignored him, instead bringing the hail on line. He began to say, *"Marquand* here," but he wasn't even able to get that much about before an upset voice said, with no preamble, "Why are you backing off?"

"We are returning to our vessel," Kebron said

flatly. "A situation has come to our attention. *Marquand* out." And with that he severed the connection.

"What are you hoping to accomplish?" demanded Si Cwan.

"Merely being cautious."

"The hell you are. This is all part of your attempt to upset me, to interfere with—"

Unperturbed, the Brikar cut him off with a terse "This solar system, like all others, does not revolve around you. I do not like that she severed communications with us. If I were a young woman, connecting with my brother who might have been dead for all I knew, I would keep talking to him until he was aboard. I wouldn't shut down the connection, as if I were afraid he might figure out that I was an impostor."

"That is—"

And then a light began to flash on the control panel, a sharp warning beep catching their attention. Kebron immediately began to bring the ship around as Si Cwan demanded, "What's happening?"

"We're being targeted. They're going to fire on us."

"They're . . . what?"

Si Cwan looked out the main window, catching a glimpse of the *Kayven Ryin* as the shuttle craft started to angle away from it. A motion on the aft section caught his attention. Despite their distance, his eyesight was formidable and he zeroed in with impressive visual acuity. What he saw were two gunports opening, and twin heavy-duty phaser cannons snapped into view. And the last thing he saw before their view of the science ship was cut off was the muzzles of the cannons flaring to life.

"Brace yourself!" shouted Kebron. "I'm trying to bring the warp drive on line before—"

He didn't have time to complete the sentence before the *Marquand* was struck amidships by the phaser cannons. The runabout spiraled out of control as Kebron fought to regain command of the battered ship. To his credit, he never lost his cool. Indeed, it might not have been within his makeup to become disconcerted.

Si Cwan was not strapped into his chair. As a result, he was tossed around the interior of the cabin, reaching out desperately to try and grab hold of something, anything, to halt himself. He crashed against one wall and felt something in his shoulder give way.

Sparks flew out of the front console as Kebron tried to institute damage procedures. The shuttle craft was rocked again, and Kebron shouted, "We have to abandon ship!"

"What?" Si Cwan was on his back, looking around, stunned and confused.

There was a gash in Si Cwan's head which Kebron hoped wasn't as bad as it looked. It wasn't going to look good in his service record if he'd left with a live passenger and returned with a corpse. The notion that the status of his record might be utterly moot didn't enter into his considerations. He was not prepared to admit that as a possibility. "Warp engines are down. We're perfect targets out here. We have to assume that they're going to keep shooting until they blow us to pieces."

"Why are they doing this?"

"As a guess: because they want to kill you. I'm simply the lucky bystander." He grabbed Si Cwan by the arm and Si Cwan howled in such agony that Kebron quickly released him. He knew he hadn't pulled on Si Cwan with any force; the mere movement of the arm had been enough to elicit the screams, and he realized that Cwan's arm was injured. "Get up!" he said, urgency entering his voice for the first time. "We have to go."

"Go where?"

"There!" Kebron stabbed a finger in the general direction of the science vessel that they had come to aid. Si Cwan was staggering to his feet and Kebron grabbed him by the back of the neck, which somehow seemed a less injurious place to hold him. He propelled him toward the two-person transporter nestled in the cockpit of the shuttle craft.

Fire was beginning to consume the main console, smoke filling up the interior of the shuttle craft. Moving with surprising dexterity considering their size, the Brikar's fingers yanked out a small panel from the wall next to the transporter, revealing a red button which he immediately punched. It was a failsafe device, provided for a situation precisely like this one, where voice recognition circuitry was failing and setting coordinates through the main console was an impossibility.

The emergency evacuation procedure was activated, an automatic five-second delay kicking in, providing Kebron and Si Cwan that much time to step onto the transporter pads. Si Cwan was nursing his injured shoulder as Kebron half pushed, half pulled him onto the pads and hoped that they actually had five seconds remaining to them.

The transporter automatically surveyed their immediate environment and locked on to the first, nearest destination that would enable them to survive. And an instant later, Si Cwan's and Zak Kebron's bodies dissipated as the miraculous transporter beams kicked in, sending their molecules hurtling through the darkness of space to be reassembled in the place that was their only hope for survival: the science vessel *Kayven Ryin.* The vessel which had assaulted them, and now provided their one chance to live . . . if only for a few more minutes, at best.

When Zoran saw the *Marquand* backing away, he began to tremble with fury. "Where are they going? We gave them what they wanted. Si Cwan spoke to his sister. Get them back here!" And he cuffed Rojam on the side of the head. "Get them back!"

Rojam barely felt the physical abuse. He was too concerned with the *Marquand* suddenly moving away from the station, as if they had tumbled to the trick. More on point, he was concerned with how Zoran was going to react, and what precisely Zoran might do to vent his displeasure. Hailing the shuttle craft, he tried to control the growing franticness he was feeling as he asked, "Why are you backing off?"

From the shuttle craft there came nothing more than a brief, to-the-point response: "We are returning to our vessel. a situation has come to our attention. *Marquand* out."

"They know! *They know!*" roared Zoran.

Rojam's mind raced as he tried to determine the accuracy of the assessment. "I . . . I don't think they do. Suspect, perhaps, but they don't know. They want to see what we'll do. If we're just cautious . . ."

"If we're cautious, then they're gone!"

"We don't know that for sure! Zoran, listen to me—!"

But listening was the last thing that Zoran had in mind. Instead, with a full-throated roar of anger, the powerfully built Thallonian knocked Rojam out of his seat. Rojam hit the floor with a yelp as Zoran dropped down at the control console. "Get away from there, Zoran!" Rojam cried out.

"Shut up! You're afraid to do what has to be done!" Even as he spoke, Zoran quickly manipulated the controls.

"I'm not afraid! But this is unnecessary! It's a mistake!"

"It's my decision, not yours! You're lucky I haven't killed you already for your incompetence!

And if the phaser cannons you rigged up don't perform as you promised . . ."

But the need to complete the threat didn't materialize, for the phaser cannons dropped obediently into position, even as their targeting sights locked onto the *Marquand.*

"In the name of all those whom you abused, Si Cwan . . . vengeance!" snarled Zoran as he triggered the firing command.

The phaser cannons let loose, both scoring direct hits, and the cries of triumph from the half-dozen Thallonians in the control room was deafening. Actually, only five of them cheered; Rojam pulled himself to sitting, rubbing the side of his head where Zoran had struck him. "This isn't necessary," he said again, but he might as well have been speaking to an empty room.

The shuttle craft was pounded by the phaser cannons, helpless before the onslaught. The Thallonians cheered every shot, overjoyed by Zoran's marksmanship. Even an annoyed Rojam had to admit that, for all his faults, Zoran was a good shot. Of course, having computers do all the work certainly helped.

"Hit them again!" crowed Dackow, the shortest and yet, when the mood suited him, loudest of the Thallonians. Dackow never voiced an opinion until he was absolutely positive about how a situation was going to go, at which point he supported the prevailing opinion with such forcefulness that it was easy to forget that he hadn't expressed a preference one way or the other until then. "You've got them cold, Zoran!"

Zoran fired again, this time missing the shuttle craft with one phaser cannon but striking it solidly with the other.

But as Zoran gleefully celebrated his marksmanship, Rojam commented dryly, "What happened to having Si Cwan's throat in your hands, enabling you to squeeze the life out of him?"

The observation brought Zoran up short for a moment. "If you had done your job better, I might have had that opportunity," he said, but it seemed a hollow comeback. The truth was that Rojam's statement had taken some of the joy out of Zoran's moment of triumph. Granted he had won, but it wasn't in the way he would have liked.

And then a flash consumed the screen as the shuttle craft erupted in a ball of flame. Automatically the Thallonians flinched, as if the explosion posed a threat to them. Within mere seconds the flame naturally burned itself out, having no air in the vacuum of space to feed it. The fragments of the vessel which had been the *Marquand* spun away harmlessly, the twisted scraps of duranium composites no longer recognizable as anything other than bits of metal.

"Burn in hell, Si Cwan," Zoran said after a long moment. The others, as always, nodded in agreement.

Only Rojam did not join in the self-congratulations. Instead he was busy checking the instrumentation on an adjoining console. "What are you doing?" asked Zoran after a moment.

"Scanning the debris," Rojam informed him.

"Why?" said Juif, making no effort to keep the sarcasm from his voice. "Are you concerned they still pose a threat?"

"Perhaps they do at that."

The pronouncement was greeted with contemptuous guffaws until Rojam added, "They weren't aboard the shuttle craft."

"What?" The comment immediately galvanized Zoran. "What are you talking about? Are you positive? It's impossible."

"It's not impossible, and they weren't there," Rojam said with growing confidence. "There's no sign of them among the debris. I wouldn't expect to find any bodies intact . . . not with the force of that explosion. But there should be *something* organic among the wreckage. I'm not detecting anything except pieces from the shuttle craft."

"Are you saying they were never aboard? That it was some sort of trick?" Zoran's anger was growing by the minute.

"That's a possibility, but I don't think so. If they were never at risk, then they went to a great deal of trouble to try and force our hand. But here is a thought: Some of those Federation shuttles come equipped with transporter pads."

"You think they may have evacuated before the ship blew up."

"Exactly."

"But the only place they could have gone to . . ." And then the growing realization brought a smile to his face. ". . . is here. Here, aboard the ship."

Rojam nodded.

Beaming with pleasure, Zoran clapped a hand on Rojam's back. "Excellent. Excellent work." Rojam let out a brief sigh of relief as Zoran turned to the others and said briskly, "All right, my friends. Somewhere in this vessel, Lord Si Cwan and his associate, Lieutenant Kebron, are hiding. Let's flush them out . . . and give our former prince the royal treatment he so richly deserves."

SELAR

III.

SOLETA GLANCED UP from her science station as she became aware that McHenry was hovering over her. She glanced up at him, her eyebrows puckered in curiosity. "Yes?" she asked.

Glancing around the bridge in a great show of making certain that no one was paying attention to them, McHenry said to her in a lowered voice, "I just wanted to say thanks."

"You're welcome," replied Soleta reasonably, and tried to go back to her studies of mineral samples extracted from Thallon.

"Don't you want to know why?" he asked after a moment.

"Not particularly, Lieutenant. Your desire to say it is sufficient for me."

"I know I was 'spacing out' earlier, like I do

sometimes, and I know that you were defending me. I just wanted to say I appreciate it."

"I was aware that your habits posed no threat to the *Excalibur*," she said reasonably. "I informed the captain and commander of that fact. Beyond that . . . what is there to say?"

"Why'd you leave, Soleta? Leave Starfleet, I mean."

The question caught her off guard. Now it was her turn to look around the bridge to make sure that no one was attempting to listen in. She needn't have worried; eavesdropping was hardly a pastime in which Starfleet personnel habitually engaged. Still, she was surprised over how uncomfortable the question made her feel. "It doesn't matter. I came back."

"It does matter. We were friends, Soleta, back at the Academy. Classmates."

"Classmates, yes. I had no friends." She said it in such a matter-of-fact manner that there was no hint of self-pity in her tone.

"Oh, stop it. Of course you had friends. Worf, Kebron, me . . ."

"Mark, this really isn't necessary."

"I think it is."

"And I say it isn't!"

If they had been trying to make sure that their conversation did not draw any undue attention, the unexpected outburst by Soleta put an end to that plan. Everyone on the bridge looked at the two of them in unrestrained surprise, attention snagged by

Soleta's unexpectedly passionate outburst. From the command chair, Calhoun asked, "Problem?"

"No, sir," said Soleta quickly, and McHenry echoed it.

"Are you certain?"

"Quite certain, yes."

"Because you seem to be having a rather strident dispute," he said, his gaze shifting suspiciously from one to the other.

"Mr. McHenry merely made a scientific observation, and I was disagreeing with it."

And now Shelby spoke up, observing, "It's rare one hears that sort of vehemence from anyone, much less a Vulcan."

"Lieutenant Soleta cares passionately about her work," McHenry said, not sounding particularly convincing.

"I see," said Calhoun, who didn't. "Mr. McHenry, time to Nelkar?"

"Twenty-seven minutes, sir," McHenry said without hesitation, as he turned away from Soleta and headed back to the conn.

Calhoun never failed to be impressed over how McHenry seemed to carry that knowledge in his head. Only Vulcans seemed nearly as capable of such rapid-fire calculations, and McHenry seemed even faster than the average Vulcan.

Which Soleta, for her part, did not seem to be. Her outburst had hardly been prompted by some sort of scientific disagreement. But Calhoun didn't feel it his place to probe too deeply into the reasons for it . . . at least not as long as he felt that his ship's safety was not at issue.

If it did become an issue, though, he would not hesitate to question Soleta and find out just what exactly had caused her to raise her voice to McHenry despite her Vulcan upbringing.

"Vulcans," he muttered to himself.

Soleta turned in her chair and looked questioningly at Calhoun. "What about Vulcans, Captain?" she asked.

He stared at her tapered ears, which had naturally zeroed in on the mention of her race, and he said, "I was merely thinking how what we need on this ship is more Vulcans."

"Vulcans are always desirable, Captain," she readily agreed, and went back to her analyses.

The main lounge on the *Excalibur* was situated on Deck 7 in the rear of the saucer section, and was informally called the Team Room, after an old term left over from the early days of space exploration. It was to the Team Room that Burgoyne 172 had retired upon hish returning to the ship. S/he had felt a certain degree of frustration since s/he had not had the opportunity to complete hish work on the *Cambon*. If there was one thing that Burgoyne disliked, it was leaving a project unfinished.

And then s/he saw another potentially unfinished project enter the Team Room. Dr. Selar had just walked in and was looking around as if hoping to find someone. Burgoyne looked around as well and saw that all of the tables had at least one occupant. Then s/he looked back at Selar and saw an ever-so-brief look of annoyance cross the Vulcan's face. That there was any readable emotion at all displayed by the Vulcan was surprising enough, and then Burgoyne realized the problem. Selar wasn't looking for someone to sit with. She was trying to find an unoccupied table.

Her gaze surveyed the room and she caught sight of Burgoyne. Burgoyne, for hish part, endeavored to stay low-key. S/he gestured in a friendly, but not too aggressive manner, and waved at the empty seat opposite hir. Selar hesitated a moment and then, with what appeared to be a profound mental sigh, approached Burgoyne. Burgoyne could not help but admire her stride: she was tall, almost regal of bearing. When Selar sat down, she kept her entire upper body straight. Her posture was perfect, her attitude unflinching.

"I believe," Selar said in her careful, measured tone, "that our first encounter was not properly handled . . . by either of us."

"I think the fault was mostly mine," Burgoyne replied.

"As do I. You were, after all, the one who was rather aggressively propositioning me. Nonetheless, it would not be appropriate to place the blame entirely on you. Doubtlessly I was insufficiently clear in making clear to you my lack of interest."

"Well, now," Burgoyne shifted a bit in hish chair, "I wouldn't call it 'aggressively propositioning' exactly."

"No?" She raised a skeptical eyebrow.

Burgoyne leaned forward and said, "I would call it . . ." But then hish voice trailed off. S/he reconsidered hish next words and discarded them. Instead s/he said, "Can I get you a drink?"

"I am certain that whatever you are having will be more than sufficient."

Burgoyne nodded, rose, disappeared behind the bar, and returned a moment later with a glass containing the same dusky-colored liquid that was in hish glass. Selar lifted it, sniffed it experimentally, then downed half the glass. It was only her formidable Vulcan self-control that prevented her from coughing it back up through her nose. "This . . . is not synthehol," she said rather unnecessarily.

S/he shook hish head. "It's called 'Scotch.' Rather difficult to come by, actually."

"How did you develop a taste for it?"

"Well," said Burgoyne, and it was obvious from the way s/he was warming to the subject that s/he had discussed this topic a number of times in the past. "About two years ago, I was taking shore leave on Argelius Two . . . a charming world. Have you ever been there?" Selar shook her head slightly and Burgoyne continued, "I was at this one pub, and it was quite a lively place, I can tell you. It was a place where the women were so . . ."

Burgoyne was about to rhapsodize about them at

length, but the look of quiet impatience on Selar's face quickly dissuaded hir. "In any event," continued Burgoyne, "I felt very much in my element. We Hermats are sometimes referred to as a rather hedonistic race. That's certainly a sweeping generalization, but not entirely without merit. In this pub, however, watching the Argelians and assorted visitors from other worlds engaging in assorted revelries and debaucheries, why . . . I felt that my humble leanings were dwarfed in comparison.

"And then my attention was drawn by one fellow seated over in a corner. A Terran, by the look of him, with hair silver as a crescent moon."

"You are attracted to him, no doubt," said Selar dryly.

"No, actually. He was a bit old for my tastes. But I was interested in him, for he seemed to be watching everything without any interest in participating. Furthermore he was wearing—believe it or not—a Starfleet uniform that hasn't been issued in years. A costume, I figured. I asked the bartender about him, and apparently he'd simply wandered in one day some weeks previously and just—I don't know— taken up residence there. He hardly ever left. So I went over and chatted with him. Asked him what he was doing there. He told me he was 'reliving old times,' as he put it. Remembering friends long gone, times left behind. He was reticent at first, but I got him talking. I have a knack for doing that."

"Indeed."

"Yes. And he seemed particularly intrigued when

I told him I was an engineer. He claimed that he was as well. Claimed, in fact, that he wrote the book on engineering."

"A man with drinks in him will claim a great many things when he seeks the attention of a pretty face," observed Selar.

Burgoyne was about to continue when s/he paused a moment and, with a grin, said, "Are you saying you think I have a pretty face?"

"I am saying that, with sufficient intoxication, anyone may seem attractive," replied Selar. "You were saying—?"

"Yes, well . . . as I said, he boasted of a great many things. Sufficiently intoxicated, as you noted. Came up with the most insane boasts. Said he was over a hundred and fifty years old, that he served with Captain Kirk . . . all manner of absurd notions. And he also had no patience at all for—how did he put it—?" And Burgoyne made a passable attempt at imitating a Scots brogue as s/he growled, " 'The wretched brew what passes for a man's drink in this godforsaken century.' He was drinking this," and Burgoyne tapped the glass of brown liquid.

"That very drink?"

"Not this specific one, of course. It was two years ago, remember. But he seemed to have a somewhat endless supply of it. We seemed to communicate quite well with one another. At first, I believe, he took me for a standard-issue female, and he openly flirted with me. When I informed him of the Hermat race and our dual gender, at first he seemed amazed and then he just laughed and said," and again Burgoyne copied the brogue, "'Ach, I would have loved to set up Captain Kirk with one of ye on a blind date. There would have been some tales to tell about that one.'" Burgoyne paused and then added, by way of explanation, "There are some who find our dual sex disturbing."

"Is that a fact," said Selar noncommittally.

"Yes." Burgoyne swirled hish drink around in the glass. "Tell me, Doctor . . . are you among them?"

"Not at all. I find *you* disturbing."

Burgoyne's smile displayed hish fangs. "I'll take that as a compliment," s/he said.

"As you wish."

"So anyway, the Terran offered me some of what he was drinking, and I tried it, and I swear to you I thought that it was going to peel the skin off the inside of my throat. I quickly realized that he was right: The stuff they've gotten us accustomed to in Starfleet is nothing compared to genuine Earth alcohol. Hell, even Hermat beverages pale in comparison to," and s/he rubbed the glass affectionately, "good ol' Scots whiskey. He told me if I had any intention of being a genuine engineer, that I should be able to drink him under the table. So I matched him drink for drink."

"And did you succeed? In drinking him under the table, I mean."

"Are you kidding?" Burgoyne laughed. "The last thing I remember was his smiling face turning at about a forty-five-degree angle . . . or at least that's what it seemed like before I hit the floor. But before that happened, I really let him have it."

" 'Have it'?"

"I told him that I thought he was being gutless. That he was sitting in this pub hiding from the rest of the galaxy, when he could be out accomplishing amazing things. That he might be telling himself that he was being nostalgic, but in fact he was just being gutless," and s/he tapped one long finger on the table three times to emphasize the last three words. Then s/he winced slightly and said, "At least I think that's what I told him. It got a little fuzzy there at the end. When I came to, I was in a back room at the pub with all sorts of debauchery and perversity going on all around me. Reminded me of home, actually. And I found that he'd left me something: a bottle of Scotch, and a message scribbled on the label of the bottle. And the message was exactly two words long: He'd written, 'You're right.' "

" 'You're right.' That was the message in its entirety."

"The whole thing, yes. Never saw him again, but I can only assume that he decided to get back out to where he belonged."

"And where would that be?"

"Damned if I know." Burgoyne leaned forward. "Do you understand what I'm saying to you, Doctor?"

"Oh. Well . . . not really, no. I had simply assumed that this was a long and fairly pointless narrative. Why? Is there something to this story beyond that?"

"What I'm saying, Selar, is that we shouldn't be afraid to try new things. We Hermats have our . . . unusual anatomical quirks. But—"

She put up a hand. "Lieutenant Commander . . ."

"An unwieldy title. I prefer Burgoyne from you."

"Very well. Commander Burgoyne . . . despite a valiant endeavor, this conversation is not proceeding in substantially different fashion than our previous one. I am not interested in you."

"Yes, you are. You simply don't know it yet."

"May I ask how you have come to this intriguing, albeit it entirely erroneous, conclusion?"

"All right . . . but only if you promise to keep it between us."

She pushed the drink of Scotch several inches away from her as she said, "I assure you, Chief Burgoyne . . . nothing will give me greater personal satisfaction than knowing that this conversation will go no further than this table."

S/he leaned forward conspiratorially and gestured that Selar should get closer to hir. With a soft sigh, Selar did as Burgoyne indicated, and the Hermat said in such a low voice that even the acute hearing of the Vulcan could barely hear hir:

"Pheromones," whispered Burgoyne.

"I beg your pardon?"

"Pheromones. Hermats can detect an elevated pheromone level in most races. It's a gift. It cues us to rising sexual interest and excitement."

"I see. And you're detecting an elevated pheromone level in me."

"That is precisely right," Burgoyne said with such confidence that even the unflappable Selar felt a bit disconcerted. "You're becoming sexually excited . . . more so when you're with me, I like to think, although that may simply be wishful thinking on my part. I have always been something of a romantic."

"Commander . . . I am certain that you are quite good at your job . . ."

"I am."

"But you are unfamiliar with Vulcan biology. It is . . ." And then she caught herself, surprise flooding through her mind. She had been about to discuss such delicate and personal matters as *Pon farr* with an offworlder. What was she thinking? Why was she having trouble prioritizing? ". . . it is impossible that I would be interested in you, in any event."

"Impossible why?"

"I cannot go into it."

Burgoyne leaned forward with a look of genuine curiosity on hish face. "Why can't you go into it?"

"I cannot," Selar said, her voice rising a bit more than she would have thought appropriate. The volume of her response didn't quite penetrate.

"Look, at the very least, I'd like to be your friend. If there's some problem that—"

And Selar was suddenly on her feet, and her response was a roar of fury. *"I said I cannot go into it! What part of 'cannot' did you not comprehend?!"*

The silence was instantaneous throughout the Team Room. Selar had managed, with no effort at all, to focus all attention in the room on herself. It was hardly a position that she desired to be in. Slowly her gaze surveyed the Team Room. Fighting to recapture her normal tone of voice, she asked, "May I assume you have something of greater importance on your minds than me?"

The crewmen needed no further urging to return to their respective conversations, although there were assorted quick glances in Selar's direction.

Automatically she put her hand to the underside of her throat. Her pulse was racing. The sounds of the room suddenly seemed magnified. Her temper had flared with Burgoyne, and although s/he might be one of the more irritating individuals that Selar had ever met, s/he was hardly enough to warrant the Vulcan tossing aside years of training and indulging in an emotional outburst.

"I have to go," she said, exerting her magnificent control over herself.

All flirtation, all smugness, was gone from Burgoyne. Instead s/he took Selar's hand firmly in hish own. Selar tried halfheartedly to pull clear, but Burgoyne's grip was surprisingly strong. Belatedly Selar remembered that Hermats had physical strength approximately two and a half times Earth norm. "Selar . . . if nothing else, we're fellow officers. If a fellow officer is in trouble, I'll do everything I can to alleviate that trouble. Whatever is wrong with you, I want to help."

"I do not need help. I merely need to be left alone. Thank you." And she exited as quickly as she could from the Team Room. This left everyone staring in confusion at Burgoyne. Burgoyne, for hish part, merely raised a glass. "May the Great Bird of the Galaxy roost on your planets," s/he said to the collective Team Room. S/he finished off the contents of hish glass and then, with a shrug, s/he reached over, picked up Selar's glass, and knocked that back, too.

Selar ran as quickly as she could down the *Excalibur* corridors. Twice she almost knocked over passing crewmen before she made it to sickbay. Upon seeing her return, Dr. Maxwell promptly proceeded to give her a quick precis on the status of the four dozen passengers from the *Cambon*. But before he could get out more than a sentence, she cut him off with a sharp gesture.

"Is there anything wrong, Doctor?" asked Maxwell, now clearly concerned about the condition of the chief medical officer. "Any problem that I can help with?"

"I am fine," she replied in a less-than-convincing manner.

"Are you sure? You seem rather flushed. Is there a—"

"Are you an expert on Vulcan physiology?" Selar demanded.

"No . . . no, not an expert per se, although I'm certainly well versed in—"

"Well, I am an expert, Doctor," she shot back. "I have been living inside my particular Vulcan physiology for quite some time now, and I assure you that I am in perfect health."

"With all due respect, Doctor, I don't know as I'd agree."

"With all due respect to *you,* Doctor, your agreement or lack thereof is of no relevance to me whatsoever." And with that she stalked quickly to her office, locking the door behind her to guarantee privacy.

She had no desire to subject herself to a medical scan in sickbay in full view of every one of her staff and technicians. She had no particular concern over the privacy of other crew members when it came to getting physicals or having problems attended to. But now that it was she herself who was in question, her right to privacy had assumed paramount importance. It was ironic, and yet an irony that she was not exactly in any condition to truly appreciate.

She opened an equipment compartment in the wall and extracted a medical tricorder. Adjusting it for herself, she began to take readings.

Pulse, heartbeat, respiration . . . everything was elevated. Moreover, she was having trouble focusing on anything.

Selar reached deep into herself. A calm, cool center of logic was drilled into Vulcans at such an early age that it became utterly ingrained into their nature. Yet Selar was having to relive that training, finding that cool center and tapping into it. Her body, her system, was entirely at the command of her mind and she would force it to obey her commands. Slowly she quieted her hurried breathing. She cleared away every noise, every distraction, until she could hear the accelerated beating of her own heart. She slowed it, bit by bit, replacing the dim red haze which seemed to have taken hold of her with a sedate, serene blue.

She thought back to her first days at the Academy, the first time that she had encountered the Academy pool. Such things were virtually unknown on Vulcan, an arid planet with a steady red sky and a sun so searing that Vulcans had even developed an inner eyelid to shield themselves against its effects. The pool might well have been an alien artifact; indeed, in many ways it was to her.

Clad in a bathing suit, she had stood on the edge of the pool, dipping a toe into it, unsure of what to do. Every logical bone in her body had told her that there was nothing to fear. That fear was besides the point, as it so often was. And yet she could not bring herself to ease herself into the water . . . until the decision had been taken out of her hands when a passing cadet named Finnegan had thought it the height of hilarity to shove her from behind into the pool. She had fallen feet-first into the deep end of the pool . . . and proceeded to drown, since naturally people who are born on a desert planet have absolutely no idea how to swim. The selfsame Finnegan, chagrined, had immediately leaped into the water and pulled out the sputtering Vulcan.

But Selar had taken that first unpleasant experience as a challenge, and every day found her at the pool until she was as good a swimmer as anyone at the Academy. Many was the time where she would simply float in the water, arms outstretched, bobbing with the gentle lapping of the water.

Now she was projecting herself back to that time. She imagined herself floating, floating ever so gently, buoyed as if by lapping waves. Bit by bit, she fashioned her recollections of the Academy pool into a place of escape. The rest of the world, her worries, her concerns, her uncharacteristic confusion, all melted away as she bobbed in the water with no distractions. She felt her composure returning to her, her ineffable logic controlling her actions once more. Whatever was happening to her, it was nothing that she couldn't control. Nothing that . . .

"Hi," said a voice. And there, swimming past her in a tight bathing suit that accentuated hish firm breasts, hish curvaceous hips, and also what seemed an impressive male endowment, was Burgoyne.

Selar snapped forward in her chair, the pool vanishing along with the Hermat intruder. She looked around and found herself, of course, still in her office. A quick scan with the medical tricorder told her that her bioreadings were back to normal. But the image of Burgoyne was solidly rooted in her mind.

She leaned forward toward her computer terminal and said, "Computer."

"Working."

"Personal medical log, Stardate 50926.2 . . ."

There was a pause, sufficiently long enough for the computer to prompt, "Waiting for entry."

Selar could only think of one thing to say, really. Five words that summarized her present situation with simple eloquence.

"I am in big trouble," she said.

KEBRON

IV.

"How much trouble would you say we're in, precisely?" Si Cwan asked in a low, tense voice.

"A good deal," replied Zak Kebron.

Between them they had precisely one phaser, the sidearm that Kebron habitually carried whenever embarking on any sort of mission. They'd had no time to grab anything else off the shuttle before the unfortunate ship had blown up.

The science vessel was not terribly large—only eight decks deep—and it was one of the oldest models of such ships. Stairs or ladders between decks instead of turbolifts, and flooring made of grated metal that made a hellacious racket whenever Kebron, in particular, walked on it. Moreover the lighting was dim. Whether it was because they were on battery backup, or had deliberately made it that way just to throw off Kebron and Si Cwan, was impossible to say.

They hunched in a corner as best they could, considering Si Cwan's height and that Kebron wasn't exactly built for hunching. "This is insane," muttered Si Cwan. "Why did they shoot at us?"

"When you're trying to kill someone, that's usually a reliable method."

"But why were they trying to kill us?"

"Immaterial. The fact of it is all we need to deal with." From the shadows that surrounded them, he was surveying the area as thoroughly as he could.

"We need a plan," Si Cwan said urgently.

Kebron appeared to consider it a moment, and then he said simply, "Survival."

"That's *obvious*. Are you being deliberately obtuse, Kebron? Our lives are at stake . . ."

Kebron glared at him, and there was extreme danger in those eyes, glittering against the dusky brown skin. *"Our* lives are at stake because *you* insisted on trying to rescue your sister. Do not forget that."

"Of course not. Now that we've properly assigned the blame, can we deal with the problem at hand?" Si Cwan waited, but the only response he got was a grunt. Taking that to be a "yes," he considered the situation a moment and then said, "I say we should split up."

"And I say you're a fool," replied Kebron.

"Why? We're less of a target that way."

Kebron scowled at him. "Look at me. Look at

you. Look at our size and build. Singly or together, we're targets. Individually, neither of us can watch each other's backs."

"As if you'd watch my back," Si Cwan snorted disdainfully. "Good luck to you, Kebron. I'll take my chances." He started to move out of the shadows, and suddenly he felt Kebron's powerful hand clamp on his shoulder. Before he could utter so much as a word of protest, Kebron had hauled him back and slammed him into the wall behind them. It shuddered slightly with the impact.

"You're not a prince here, Cwan," Kebron said tightly. "You're not a lord. You will do what I say, when I say it, or so help me I'll crush your head with my bare hands and save whoever's out to get us the trouble. Do we understand each other?"

There were a hundred responses that Si Cwan wanted to make, but he choked them all down . . . which wasn't especially difficult, since he was choking from the grip that Kebron had on him. So all he managed to get out was a very hoarse whisper of, "Perfectly."

Kebron released him and Si Cwan rubbed the base of his throat as he glared at Kebron. "You're supposed to be on *my* side?"

Zak Kebron didn't bother to dignify the question with an answer. Instead he was listening. "Here they come," he said slowly, his voice dropping to nearly a whisper.

Si Cwan was listening as well. "Two of them. Do you think that's all there are?"

"Safer to assume it's not," observed Kebron, and this was a sentiment that Si Cwan couldn't disagree with.

Kebron pointed silently upward, indicating that he was hearing them from overhead. Si Cwan nodded, and then he looked behind them. Ten feet to the rear was a stairway angling to the upper floor, with spaces between the steps. Cwan chucked a thumb in the direction of the stairs, and Kebron immediately intuited what Si Cwan had in mind. They dropped back and tried to duck behind the stairs, but the space was too narrow for the both of them to fit. Kebron pointed a finger at Si Cwan and said, "Decoy."

Being a decoy was not exactly Si Cwan's first choice of responsibilities, but there was no time to argue the point. Besides, there was something in the challenging way that Kebron looked at him that angered him. As if Kebron was certain that Si Cwan would never present danger to himself and trust Kebron to bail him out of it.

Si Cwan took up a station directly in front of the stairs, standing about five feet back. Kebron took up a position behind the stairs. There was clattering from overhead and then two pairs of feet descended the stairs. Cwan gasped when he saw that they were two Thallonians. They slowed as they came within view of Si Cwan. Each of them was cradling a strange-looking weapon that Si Cwan didn't recognize at first, but then he did. They were plasma blasters, and there were few weapons in existence that were nastier.

The two of them stopped several steps above the floor. "Where's the other one, Si Cwan?" demanded one of the Thallonians. "The one with the voice like rumbling thunder."

"He died during the first bombardment of your ambush," replied Si Cwan. "He didn't make it off the ship."

"Now, why don't I believe you?" asked one of the Thallonians. "Are you trying to deceive us, Si Cwan?"

"Where is my sister? Who are you?" he demanded.

They hadn't budged from their place on the stairs. "You are in no position to ask quest—" one of them started to say.

Where is my sister, and who are you?" There was a dark, fearsome tone to his voice, and the Thallonians found themselves shuddering to hear it. Once upon a time, to hear such a tone would be tantamount to a death sentence. Even though the unarmed Si Cwan was staring down the barrels of weapons aimed squarely at him from point-blank distance, it seemed as if he was the one who was in charge.

"My name is Skarm," one of them finally said, and he indicated the Thallonian standing next to him with a nod of his head. "And this is Atol. It is only fitting, I imagine, that you know the name of the ones who are about to kill you. As for your sister," and Skarm smiled lopsidedly, "that's for us to know."

He touched a small button on the side of the plasma blaster and took a step down. He aimed it squarely at Si Cwan, and the former prince merely stood there, dark eyes sparkling with cold fury.

And Zak Kebron's hands snaked out from underneath the steps, grabbing Skarm's ankles. Skarm, confused as to what was happening, let out an alarmed yelp, his arms pinwheeling as he tried to halt his forward plummet. He didn't succeed and he crashed forward, even as the one called Atol frantically tried to figure out what had just happened.

The blaster tumbled out of Skarm's hand and clattered to the floor. Si Cwan lunged for it and Atol immediately fired off a shot from his own blaster. It was like having a weapon that fired molten lava. The plasma blast stream blew directly in front of Si Cwan, and only Cwan's speed saved him as he ducked backward. The stream hit the fallen weapon, immediately rupturing the cartridge that contained the plasma field.

Si Cwan had a split second to react, and he did the only thing he could think to do. He leaped straight up, fingers desperately grabbing the grillework of the rampway directly above him, and he swung his body upward just as the crippled gun exploded. A stream of flame ripped right beneath him, and he could feel the back of his jacket catch on fire. Instantly he shucked the jacket, allowing it to drop into the flames beneath him, and he felt them licking at him hungrily.

Atol was blistered by the heat, but even so he tried to look down beneath the steps. He had only a split-second warning as he saw the terrible eyes of Zak Kebron, and then Kebron—disdaining the subtle approach—smashed upward, tearing the stairs out of their moorings and sending Atol pitching forward into the flames of the burning plasma. Skarm rolled off the steps as Kebron shoved them upward, and it was clear from the lolling of his head that he was already dead. When he'd fallen, he'd snapped his neck.

Atol let out a truncated shriek as the flame consumed him. It had all happened within the space of a few seconds, and then the ship's automatic firefighting defenses kicked in. High-powered spray hissed out from hidden pipes lining the sides of the corridor, battling the flames and quickly extinguishing them.

Si Cwan dropped to the ground, landing in a crouch. Kebron tossed aside the twisted remains of the stairs as Cwan went immediately to the fallen Atol. Atol's body was a mass of burns: the plasma had done its work quickly, efficiently, and horribly. Clearly he was done for, but Si Cwan was not inclined to let him depart quite that easily. He grabbed Atol by the side of the head, yanking him upward. This did him no good, as the skin he was gripping peeled off in his hand, no more than a large, blackened, and charred fistful of flesh. With a grunt of disgust, Si Cwan tossed it aside and elected instead to snarl into Atol's face, "Where is my sister? Is she on this vessel? Who's behind this? If you have any hope of greeting your ancestors with a shred of integrity—the ancestors who swore fealty to my bloodline before the birth of your father's father's father—then answer my questions *now!*"

Atol's mouth moved, but no word emerged. However, Si Cwan could still make out what Atol was saying, even without sound. A two-syllable name that he'd hoped not to hear ever again. "Zoran?" he said with dread.

Atol managed, just barely, to nod, and then his body began to tremble. "Go to your ancestors," Si Cwan told him, and as if obeying a final order from his former liege, Atol's head shook—although whether in compliance or from final spasms, it was impossible to tell. And then his eyes rolled up into the top of his head.

Kebron stood over the two fallen Thallonians, looking at his handiwork. His phaser was still snugly in its holster, untouched. "I was under the impression," Si Cwan said, "that Starfleet security officers usually give people the option of surrendering."

The Brikar appeared to consider that a moment as he nudged Skarm's body with the toe of his boot. Then he replied, "Ugly rumors." He paused, and then asked, "Who is Zoran?"

"A very unusual man. He's someone who wants to kill me."

Kebron looked at him and, with the famed Brikar

deadpan, said, "I hope you don't think that wanting to kill you makes him unusual."

Si Cwan grunted in a tone that almost indicated morbid amusement, and then he stepped past Kebron. Cwan was a natural leader, and his tendency was to take the point, to be in the forefront, during any situation.

This time it almost cost him his life.

Kebron only noticed at the last second that a shadow was separating from other shadows farther down the hallway. The two had been accompanied by a third, and he'd come down and around while the first two were engaging them by the stairway. Zak only had a moment to react. With a sweep of his massive arm he knocked Si Cwan to the floor, yanking his phaser clear and firing . . .

. . . not in time. The assailant at the far end of the hallway saw the phaser being brought to bear on him, and he dodged under the beam even as he fired off a shot with the plasma blaster. The blaster struck Kebron in the upper right shoulder, and the Brikar let out a pained grunt, which was the most he would do to acknowledge pain. With any other species, the plasma would have torn off the shoulder right down to the bone. The Brikar's hide was considerably tougher than that. Even so, the Brikar was clearly in pain, the plasma sizzling on his shoulder and the ghastly smell of burning flesh filling the air.

He dropped his phaser, and Si Cwan snatched it out of midair. He caught it, aimed, and fired in one smooth motion, and the phaser blasted the Thallonian assailant back. He smashed against the far wall, the plasma blaster spinning out of his hand, falling to his side. Clutching his chest, the Thallonian tried to lunge for the blaster, but then he saw that Si Cwan was targeting him again, and he leaped away in the other direction, disappearing down a cross corridor before Si Cwan could nail him with a phaser shot. Si Cwan charged after him, not even stopping to check on the condition of the fallen Brikar. His focus was entirely on catching up with this latest assailant and finding out whether or not Kalinda was anywhere on the ship. Even if he had to beat it out of him, he was going to find out.

He rounded the corner, not even stopping to pick up the plasma blaster, because he was in such a hurry to catch up with the Thallonian. There was no sign of him, and Si Cwan moved around another corner and started down another corridor.

He never even saw the iron bar that lashed out. But he felt it as it slammed into the arm that was holding the phaser. To his credit he held on to it and he tried to bring it up to bear on his attacker, but another swing of the bar crunched his fingers and knocked the phaser out of his hand.

"Afraid to face me man-to-man, O great lord?" taunted the Thallonian. The bar he was holding was about three feet long, and he was gripping it firmly at the base.

"I know you. Dackow, isn't it," Si Cwan said slowly. One of his hands was throbbing, but the other was functioning just fine, and his fingers curled around the floor grating beneath him. He felt a bit of give in the flooring, and realized that it wasn't one solid piece, but instead fitted in sections, the edges of the crisscrossed metal fitting neatly into slots in the base of the hallway flooring.

Dackow paused, surprised. "I'm impressed that such a great man as yourself would remember a humble nothing such as me."

"It's difficult to forget someone quite as sycophantic as you. As I recall, you preferred to hover around the fringes of the great court, laughing at the right times when the right people spoke, scowling when others fell out of favor. And when the tide turned against my family, you were one of the first to switch to the side of those who wanted us out. You bend with the wind, Dackow, and doubtlessly congratulate yourself over your foresight, when the fact is that you're just a coward. A coward through and through."

With a roar of fury, Dackow drew the bar back over his head and swung it down in a fierce arc. Had it landed, it would have caved in Si Cwan's skull.

With a quick twist, Si Cwan ripped the metal flooring out from under himself and held it up as a shield. The bar crashed into the grating, the reverberation of the metal almost deafening. Dackow switched angles and tried to strike Si Cwan across the ribs. Again, no good. Si Cwan intercepted it, down on one knee. Again and again, fury building with every stroke, Dackow tried to slam his bar into the Thallonian prince. Left, right, up and down, and every time Si Cwan blocked it.

Dackow, with a roar of rage, reversed his grip on the bar and tried to drive it downward as if staking a vampire. Si Cwan backrolled, putting a short distance between himself and Dackow, and then he threw the flooring as if it were a discus. Dackow saw it coming, but there was no room in the narrow corridor to get out of the way. The grating lanced into him with tremendous force, the edges driving into his solar plexus. Dackow howled in pain and Si Cwan was on his feet, his powerful legs thrusting him forward, his hands outstretched. He caught the edges of the grating and shoved as hard as he could. The force of the lunge drove the edging of the grating right into Dackow, penetrating half a foot, and the charge lifted Dackow off his feet. His back crashed into the wall and there was an audible snap . . . the sound of his spine breaking, as if being impaled wasn't enough.

Blood poured from his mouth as Si Cwan stepped back, releasing his grip on the grating and allowing Dackow to fall to the ground. "Where is Kalinda? Where is my sister?" demanded Si Cwan.

Dackow gathered some of the blood that was pouring from his mouth, and managed to transform it into a contemptuous spit which he hurled at Si Cwan. It was the last thing he would ever do.

There was a heavy step behind Si Cwan and he whirled, his arms in a defensive position, but it was only Kebron standing behind him. The Brikar was massaging his damaged shoulder as he said, *"First* question . . . *then* kill. More productive."

"I'll try to keep that in mind," shot back Si Cwan. He stood, feeling momentarily shaky. The wear and tear of the running fight was beginning to take its toll. "How many more do you think there are?"

"I have no idea," replied Kebron. "That's what bothers me." He picked up the fallen phaser, returned it to its holster. He was cradling one of the plasma blasters and pointed out the other one, which had fallen. "Grab it and let's go."

Earlier, Si Cwan might have been annoyed at the commanding tone of Kebron's voice. But now he simply nodded and picked up the fallen plasma blaster. "I don't generally like weapons," he commented. "They can malfunction or be taken from you."

"Really. I'm the same way. Use them if I have to, though." He pointed with authority. "That way."

"Why that way?"

"Why not?"

Having no ready answer, Si Cwan shrugged and they headed off in the direction that Kebron had indicated. But then they heard a small, high-pitched sound from behind them. They stopped, turned . . .

. . . and realized that Dackow was beeping.

In the control center, Zoran was staring at Rojam in disbelief. "You can't raise *any* of them?"

Rojam shook his head. "I've lost contact with all

three of them. They're not responding on the comm links at all."

"Three armed Thallonian ravagers against a single Starfleet fool and an effete snob," snarled Zoran. "How is it possible?"

And Rojam lost patience with Zoran, which was a very dangerous thing for him to do, but he no longer cared. "Because Starfleet is not composed of fools, Zoran, and because Si Cwan—for all that you dislike him, for all that any of us dislikes him—is anything but an effete snob. He's as formidable a warrior as they come, and you'd do well to remember that."

"I would do well to remember that? I would do well? And you would do well," snarled Zoran, his hands flexing in fury, "would do well to remember—"

He didn't have the chance to finish the sentence, however, because the comm panel beeped. Rojam punched the link-up, noting the identifier assigned to it, and said, "Dackow? Progress?"

There was a pause, and then a familiar voice said, "Dackow isn't making much progress at the moment." They could hear a soft chuckle, and then: "Hello, Zoran."

Low and angry, Zoran snarled, "Si Cwan."

"It has been a long time, hasn't it."

"I'll kill you for this."

"For this and for every other imagined insult." He'd sounded amused, but then he became deadly serious. "Where is Kalinda, Zoran? She has done nothing to you. And you are nothing but a sadistic pig." His tone became mocking. "I would have thought you'd release her so that this could be between us, Zoran. Between men, without the threat of a girl's welfare overshadowing it. You always held yourself up to such a 'high' standard. Always thought yourself so much better than I. And this is how low you have fallen, consumed by your jealousy and anger. Posturing and presenting yourself as some superior individual, when you don't have the courage to—"

"She's dead, you idiot!"

Rojam turned and looked in shocked disbelief at Zoran, and for once Zoran couldn't blame him. The phantom of Kalinda had been an upper hand that they would have been able to wield against Si Cwan. Perhaps force him into some situation where he couldn't possibly get away. But he had now tossed that aside.

Zoran turned away and Rojam suspended the transmission, crossing quickly over to Zoran. "Why did you do that? Why?" he demanded.

Zoran whirled to face him and hissed, "Because I want to hurt him. I want him to die inside first. You heard him! Heard his insults, his smugness—"

"He was baiting you and you fell for it! We had an advantage! We could have made demands on him! Instead you've removed that!"

"We have an advantage! We're armed! There's more of us! There's—"

But now Juif stepped forward and pointed out,

"They're likely armed, too. We have to assume they took weapons off the others. They're roaming the ship, and they're very much in a position to hurt us."

Zoran, with apparent effort, focused on Juif. "What are you saying?"

"I'm saying we cut our losses, abandon the vessel, and blow it up from a safe distance."

"And let him get away?"

"We were never supposed to capture him! He was never part of the plan!" Juif said. "You've lost sight of that! You've lost sight of everything because Si Cwan wandered into the middle of all this, and suddenly your priorities changed! Well, my priorities are to get out of this insanity in one piece! And if that isn't yours, then there's something wrong with you."

"Wrong with me?"

"Yes!"

A calm seemed to descend upon Zoran, and truthfully the calm was more frightening than the anger. "Ten minutes," he said.

Rojam and Juif looked at each other. "What?" asked Rojam.

"Ten minutes. I want ten minutes to hunt the bastard down. If I don't have his head in ten minutes, we do as you suggest. How say you?"

The truth was that neither of them was especially enthused with the plan. But they saw the cold look in his eyes and realized that this was the best they were going to get. Slowly, and reluctantly, they nodded in agreement.

"Rojam," said Zoran, sounding almost supernaturally calm, "set a bomb for fifteen minutes. That will allow me the ten minutes to which we've agreed, and another five to get to our vessel and clear the area. More than enough."

More than enough for someone with a death wish . . . Rojam thought, but he didn't dare say it aloud. He had the feeling that he'd already gotten away with saying more than he would have thought possible.

"She's dead, you idiot!"

The words lanced through Si Cwan's heart, chilled his soul. He didn't even realize that he was wavering slightly until he felt Kebron's hand on his arm, steadying him. His red face became dark crimson, as it was wont to do when he was truly upset. He was gripping the comm unit they'd lifted off the fallen Thallonian, gripping it so tightly that he was on the verge of breaking it.

"Si Cwan . . . calm down," Kebron said forcefully. "I need you calm. They're trying to make you angry. Anger will put you at risk. At the very least, it will make you less useful to me."

It was impossible to tell whether Si Cwan heard him or not. He snarled into the comm unit, "You're lying! *You're lying!"*

There was no response and he shook the comm

unit furiously until Kebron forcibly pried it out of his hands, even as he said, "You're wasting your time. He's not responding."

Si Cwan spun to face the Brikar, and there was murder in his eyes. Kebron had felt mostly disdain for Si Cwan since they'd met. Disdain, annoyance, anger. Never, however, had he felt the least bit intimidated. The Brikar, with their massive build and the confidence that came from having as sturdy hide as they did, tended to make them rather hard to scare. When Kebron looked into Si Cwan's eyes at that moment, however, he was not exactly scared. But he knew beyond any question that he would most definitely not want to be this Zoran individual.

"We're going to find him," Si Cwan said tightly. "We're going to find him and when I kill him, Kebron, understand: I cannot use this," and he indicated the plasma blaster. "He must die with my hands on his throat. No other means will be acceptable."

"There are alternatives to killing him," Kebron told him.

The temperature in the corridor dropped about twenty degrees from the chill of Cwan's voice alone. "No. There are not."

And suddenly the comm unit beeped. Kebron tapped it and they heard Zoran's voice say, "Hello, Si Cwan. I assume you can hear me."

Si Cwan was about to snap out a harsh response, but Kebron put a finger to his lips. At first Cwan was confused, but then he realized the wisdom in this course. Conversation with Zoran would only cause Si Cwan to become angrier, more inclined to lose his temper, and that would simply give Zoran even more confidence. Cwan had to forcibly bite down on his lower lip, and several drops of blackish blood dripped out.

"Si Cwan," Zoran was saying slowly, "you were so easy to fool. All I had to do was reprogram the computer to synthesize her voice. Only took thirty seconds. Thirty seconds to get your hopes up." His voice dropped. It sounded like an obscene purr. "She died crying your name, Si Cwan. Over and over, she called for you. I won't tell you how she died. I won't tell you what was done to her, or how long it took, or any details at all. Do you know why? Because you'll envision every worst-case possibility. I wouldn't want to take the chance of the truth being less severe than whatever you might conjure up in your imagination."

Si Cwan was visibly trembling. It was all he could do to contain himself.

"I'm looking for you, Si Cwan," came Zoran's taunting voice. "Come and find me . . . if you can." And he shut off the comm link.

"Si Cwan . . . Get a grip." Kebron saw that Si Cwan was inarticulate with fury, and he gripped him firmly by the shoulders.

His voice was a strangled whisper. "I'll kill him . . ."

"If I were you, I would, too. No question. But right now, in your state of mind, he'll kill you first.

Again, no question. You're giving him exactly what he wants: a target who's out of control." But Si Cwan wasn't hearing him. He was completely internalized, muttering to himself, not at all relating to their environment. His head was filled with the imagined dying screams of his sister. Kebron shook him and said, "Cwan, I know how you feel."

With effort, Si Cwan focused on him. "No, you don't . . . you can't . . ."

"Oh yes I can," Kebron shot back. "My parents, on a mining colony . . . killed by Orion pirates who stripped the colony, looking for anything they could steal. They worked to send me to the Academy, and while I was there, their dedication was repaid with murder. And when I heard, I took leave from the Academy and tracked the pirates down. And you know what? I almost got killed. When Starfleet reps caught up with me, I was near death. I was in the hospital for two months while they put me back together. I never caught up again with the ones who destroyed my family, and I was lucky to survive the encounter, all because I was blinded by rage, just like you are now. Now snap out of it."

It was the longest speech Si Cwan could ever recall Kebron making. For that matter, it was the longest speech Kebron himself could recall making. And he had to keep on speaking quickly, while he had Si Cwan's attention. "This Zoran . . . tell me all about him. Tell me what to expect."

"Zoran . . ." Si Cwan took a deep breath. "Zoran . . . he'll probably have company, besides the ones we already disposed of. One named Rojam, the other named Juif. They're a trio."

"How do you know?"

"Because," Si Cwan said coldly, "we used to be a quartet." He paused a heartbeat. "Have you ever had to kill your best friend? Is that in our mutually shared experience as well?"

"No," admitted Kebron.

"Well . . . good," and Si Cwan gripped Zak Kebron by the elbow. "Come along, then. I'll show you how it's done."

V.

"Isn't it amazing?" murmured Calhoun, as the planet Nelkar rotated below them. He gazed at it upon the screen. "One planet looks so much like another when you're up here. Sometimes you want to take planetbound races who are at war with each other, bring them up here, show them their world. Make them realize that it's one world that they should all be sharing, rather than fighting over it."

From her position next to him on the bridge, Shelby asked, "And if someone had done that for young . . ." She hesitated over the pronunciation, as she always did, gargling it slightly, "M'k'n'zy of Calhoun . . . would he have stopped fighting?"

"No," he said with amused admission. He thought of the short sword mounted on the wall of his ready room. "Mr. Boyajian," he said in a slightly louder voice, deliberately changing subjects, "have you raised the planet's surface yet?"

"Not yet, sir. As of this point, I'm . . . Wait. Receiving transmission now."

"On screen."

The screen wavered ever so slightly, and then a male Nelkarite appeared. He had much the same angelic look as Laheera did . . . that same "too good to be true" appearance that Calhoun had felt so annoying when they'd first encountered the Nelkarites.

"Greetings," he said in a musical voice evocative of Laheera's. "I am Celter, governor of the capital city of Selinium. Welcome to Nelkar."

"Mackenzie Calhoun, captain of the *Excalibur*. Laheera informed us that you were willing to provide sanctuary for the passengers we have aboard."

"That is so. And she informed us," and clear amusement tinged his features, "that you did not trust us."

"It is my duty to be judicious when making first contacts," Calhoun said reasonably. "I would be remiss if I did not have at least some concerns with depositing four dozen people on an alien world."

"I remind you, Captain, that *you* are the aliens here. If anyone has the right to be concerned, it is we. Yet we welcome you, trust you. We would like to think that we should be accorded, at the very least, similar consideration."

"Point taken," said Calhoun. "Nonetheless, if it is all the same to you, we will send an escort down with our passengers. I'd prefer a firsthand report of the environment where we're dropping them off."

"As you wish, Captain," said Celter with polite indifference. "We have nothing to hide. We are merely doing our best to be altruistic. These are, after all, unusual times."

"All times are unusual, Governor. Some are just more unusual than others. Please send us the coordinates for an away team, and we will prepare your new residents for landfall. Calhoun out." The screen blinked off before Celter could say anything else.

And then, before Calhoun could give any order, make any pronouncement, Shelby said crisply, "Captain, request permission to head the away team, sir."

The request stopped Calhoun in midthought, and he turned to Shelby. One look into those deep purple eyes of his, and Shelby instantly knew that her surmise had been correct: Calhoun had intended to lead the away team himself, despite Starfleet's policies to the contrary. Had he voiced the composition of the away team before she'd said anything, she would have had to try and talk him into changing his mind after already speaking it. She had no desire to get into a contest of wills with him; by the same token, she had every intention of fulfilling her obligations as first officer of the *Excalibur*. And one of those obligations was to spearhead away teams so that the captain could remain safe within the confines of the bridge.

All this was conveyed by a silent look passing

between the two. It was so subtle, so understated, that it went past everyone else on the bridge. Calhoun knew Shelby's mind, and she knew his. He knew precisely why she had jumped in, and he didn't seem particularly appreciative of it. By the same token, he was also aware that she was trying to be respectful of his position and feelings. She had volunteered in such a way that her presence on the away team could now come across as a snap command decision by Calhoun, rather than a point of order over which the two of them would have to argue.

Slowly he said, "Very well. Commander Shelby, you'll take an away team composed of yourself, Lieutenant Lefler, and Security Officer Meyer."

Robin Lefler looked up from her station. "Me, sir?"

"I want an assessment on their level of technology. Your engineering background makes you the appropriate choice. Plus you finished in the top three percentile of your class in First Contact Procedures at the Academy."

She blinked in surprise, clearly impressed by her captain's apparent command over the minutiae of her academic career. Even she didn't remember exactly where she'd ranked in that one particular class. "Uhm . . . yes, sir." She rose from her station, and Boyajian, a solid "utility player" on the bridge, stepped in to take her place. She headed out at Shelby's side.

"Captain," McHenry said the moment they were

gone, "how did you know that Lefler scored so high in the F.C. Pro class?"

Calhoun smiled. "I didn't. But who's going to deny doing well in a class?"

"Captain."

He turned to face Soleta, who had just spoken. "Yes, Lieutenant?"

"Dr. Selar would like me to come down to sickbay."

"Are you ill, Lieutenant?"

"Not to my knowledge, sir. I'm not entirely certain why she wants to see me. She just now contacted me privately over my comm badge. I assume it is some sort of personal matter. Permission to leave the bridge?"

Calhoun considered it a moment, wondering whether he should go directly to Selar and ask after her. But something told him to keep a distance from the situation. "You're asking my permission for something as simple as leaving the bridge?"

"Regulations state, sir, that during a time of contact or in the midst of a mission, all hands are to remain on station and must request permission for any reason if—"

"I know the regs, Lieutenant, but the person who wrote them isn't here. You're a big girl, Soleta. Just tell me you're going and don't drop your comm badge down the commode or something so I can't reach you."

"Sir, leaving the bridge."

"Have a nice trip."

She headed into the turbolift and Calhoun sighed inwardly. What was going to be next? Shouting "Captain on the bridge!" whenever he set foot into the place? Part of him appreciated the endeavors to have respect for proper procedures. By the same token, he had seen people follow procedures so rigidly that others had died because of it. Died needlessly.

An inner voice warned him not to dwell on it excessively, for that way lay madness. And so he turned his attention back to the planet that was spinning below them.

He felt the hair on the back of his neck rising.

He didn't like the feel of this one bit.

The *Excalibur* didn't have the facilities to beam all four dozen passengers from the *Cambon* down at one time. So they were sent down in groups of six, with Shelby, Lefler, and Meyer in the first group. Meyer was slim but wiry, and he had piercing blue eyes that seemed to take in everything that was happening around them. He also had the fastest quick-draw on the ship.

Lefler immediately began studying the architecture of Selinium, as well as recording her observations on her tricorder. They had materialized in what appeared to be a main square of the city. They were standing on an upper walkway, constructed above roadways upon which traffic was moving at a brisk clip. Lefler noticed that the vehicles were strictly low-tech, moving on wheels rather than any sort of antigrav or mag-lev basis.

The city towered all around them. However, it was not a particularly large place, which was unusual considering it had been mentioned as the capital. In point of fact, the initial scans of Selinium didn't seem to indicate more than a hundred thousand people residing there, which was—relatively speaking—puny.

Still, there was something about the buildings that seemed . . . off a bit. Lefler promptly began scanning them. She was so involved in it that she didn't even see the welcome party approach the away team, and didn't look up until she heard Shelby say, "Hello. I'm Commander Shelby, *U.S.S. Excalibur.* Captain Laheera, as I recall."

Laheera, flanked by several other officials, bobbed her head in acknowledgment. " 'Captain' would be more your term than ours. The more accurate equivalent would a term along the lines of 'First Among Equals.' But 'Captain' will suffice, if you are comfortable with that."

Lefler was struck by the fact that Laheera was relatively short. Indeed, of the group of them, none of them was much above five feet tall. And yet there was something about them, some sort of inner light that made them appear—it was hard to say—bigger than they actually were. Bigger, more impressive . . . *some*thing.

Certainly her clothing did not leave much to the

imagination. As opposed to the more "official" look of the outfit she'd worn when they first saw her, Laheera was now dressed completely in clinging white: a tight white top with a hem just below her hip, and white leggings under them. The cloth adhered so closely to the line of her figure that Shelby had to look twice to ascertain whether it was, in fact, body paint. It wasn't, but it certainly could have been.

Shelby made quick introductions, and then found that Captain Hufmin of the *Cambon* was hovering nearby. He had been one of the first to come down, concerned with making sure that his charges were being properly attended to. Although Shelby could tell, from the slightly panting way that he was looking at Laheera, that there had been more to Hufmin's cooperative attitude than merely wishing to honor the desires of his passengers. He was clearly taken by the indisputable beauty of their hosts. And considering Laheera's current ensemble, his interest was on the rise. Laheera could likely have asked him to stick a phaser in his mouth and pull the trigger, and he would gratefully have complied, with his last words being profound thanks for the honor of serving her.

Lefler, meantime, turned her attention back to her duties while the introductions were being made. Shelby sidled up to her as Laheera, along with her associates, moved beyond them to meet and greet the rest of the refugees, who were continuing to beam down.

"Opinions, Lieutenant?" asked Shelby.

"Commander . . . you're familiar with the Borg, as I recall."

"A bit," Shelby said dryly.

"Well . . . this place reminds me of them a little bit, in that the Borg have . . . what's the word . . . ?"

"Assimilated?" suggested Shelby . . . always a good word when discussing the Borg.

"Right. Assimilated technology from throughout the galaxy. The thing is, the Borg have integrated it smoothly into one, uniform whole. Here, it's . . . it's a hodgepodge. Look around you." She indicated the buildings. "Everything's just sort of strewn together, with no rhyme or reason. You can't get any sense for the character of the environment. Over there, for instance," and she pointed. "Look at the dome of that building."

"What about it?" said Shelby, but then she slowly started to answer her own question. "Wait a minute . . . isn't that . . . ?"

"Andorian, yes. You can tell by the markings along the lower rim."

"What's a dome from an Andorian building doing here?"

"There's an abandoned Andorian colony on the border of Sector 221-G. My guess is that at some point, the Nelkarites picked it clean. They took whatever caught their interest. That person over there, with Laheera? Wearing a cloak of Tellarite design. That gold iris-eye door fitted into that building over there? It's off an Orion slave ship. This place is like a giant jigsaw puzzle. It's like," and she tried to find the right comparison. "It's like walking into a cannibals' village and finding clothes or trinkets taken from previous . . . uh . . . meals."

"Are you saying we have to worry about becoming the Nelkarites' consuming interest?" Shelby said slowly. She noticed that Laheera and the others had finished greeting the refugees, and were now heading back toward herself and Lefler.

Lefler seemed to consider the notion for a moment, but then she discarded it. "No . . . no, I don't think so. They just seem interested in technology, that's all. I don't think there's anything particularly dangerous about them. They're just a small, scrappy race, trying to make use of whatever they happen to get their hands on, for the purpose of getting ahead. I'll wager they even cobbled together the ship we confronted."

"Yes, Soleta made the same observation. Not saying it was 'cobbled together,' but it seemed to be a patchwork of other technology, most conspicuously Kreel."

"It's possible that Kreel raiders tried to show up here to take advantage of them . . . and paid for it with their ship."

"Which means that the Nelkarites are fully capable of protecting themselves," Shelby mused. "Certainly that's good news for the refugees. They could use some protection."

"Commander," came Laheera's musical voice. "Did I hear you saying something about . . . protection?" She seemed almost amused by the notion. "Certainly you don't think we pose a threat to you?"

Captain Hufmin sauntered up on the tail end of the comment, and before Shelby could say anything, he announced confidently, "Oh, I doubt that Commander Shelby ever thought such a thing. Right, Commander?"

Shelby smiled noncommittally. "I'm rather curious, Laheera," she said. "We're depositing four dozen refugees on you. Where do you intend to put them?"

"Oh, that's not a problem at all. I'm glad you asked that, in fact," and indeed Laheera seemed more than glad. She seemed delighted out of all proportion to the question. "We have some wonderful facilities which we've prepared."

"Not some sort of camps or something equally uninviting, I trust?"

"Not at all, Commander." Laheera leaned forward, sounding almost conspiratorial. "They're so luxurious that you might want to stay on yourself instead of returning to the *Excalibur.*"

Doing a fair impression of Laheera's almost giddy, singsong voice, Shelby replied with faux excitement, "That's a chance I'm willing to take." Lefler put a hand to her mouth to cover her own laughter, although the slight shaking of her shoulders betrayed her amusement.

"Come," said Laheera, and then she waved to the refugees who were congregating in the square, looking around in wonderment at their new home. "Come along, all of you. I'll show you to your residences." She turned back to Shelby and said, clearly pleased with herself, "And then you can return to your captain and let him know that your people are in safe hands." As she spoke, she hooked her arm through Hufmin's and together they sauntered off.

Shelby and Lefler exchanged looks.

"I think I'm going to be ill," said Lefler.

VI.

"I BELIEVE I AM ILL. Mentally ill. And I require your services to ascertain that."

Dr. Selar and Lieutenant Soleta were in Selar's private quarters. Soleta had reported to sickbay as Selar had requested, but as soon as she was there the Vulcan doctor immediately decided that her office did not provide sufficient seclusion, and so she had requested that they relocate the meeting.

Soleta was impressed at how utterly stark Selar's quarters were. It was as if she didn't really live there; as if her entire life were sickbay, and her quarters was simply where she retired to in order to attend to the minimal requirements necessary to her perpetuation. There was her computer (standard issue), her bed (standard issue) . . .

. . . and a single light.

The fact that there was nothing else in the room to draw her attention naturally prompted Soleta to focus on it. It was tall, about a foot high, and cylindrical, and shimmered with a blue radiance. She found something unutterably sad about it, and she couldn't exactly figure out why. Why would a light have a sadness about it?

Selar saw what had drawn her attention. She didn't smile, of course, or frown, or in any way evince any emotion. "You have not seen a Shantzar? A Memory Lamp?"

"No, I . . . have not," Soleta said. "A tribute of sorts?"

"Of sorts, yes. To someone . . . long gone." Briskly, she turned to Soleta and said, "I am in a . . . somewhat difficult position. I must ask your indulgence, not only as a crew woman, but as a fellow Vulcan . . . indeed, the only other Vulcan on this vessel. I ask . . ." She cleared her throat. "I formally ask you to grant me Succor."

Soleta was not quite as skilled as Selar when it came to covering her surprise. "A formal request? You could not simply ask for my help, and assume that I would give it?"

She looked downward. It was surprising to Soleta that Selar was having trouble meeting her direct gaze. "We speak of delicate matters and uncertainties. I do not wish to impose on friendship."

"Are we friends?"

"Not to my knowledge," said Selar. "That is the point."

"I cannot say I understand, because that would be lying."

Selar looked around her cabin, looked anywhere except at Soleta. "I do not . . . interact well with others," she said after a time.

"A curious admission for a doctor to make," Soleta couldn't help but observe.

Another might have taken that as a criticism, but Selar merely nodded in acknowledgment. "As a doctor, I do not see myself interacting with individuals, but rather with their ailments. It is no more necessary to make an emotional investment in patients than it is for an engineer to bond with a power coupling. If it breaks, it is my job, my vocation, to repair it. That is all."

"But engineers do bond, do they not?" asked Selar. "Humans in particular. They tend to invest inanimate objects with a sense of life. They even ascribe genders to their vessels, calling them 'she.'"

"Granted. It gives them . . . comfort, I would imagine. Humans are frequently in need of comfort." She looked imperiously at Soleta. "Vulcans are not. That is one of the elements which has been our greatest strength."

And with a sigh, Soleta replied, "Or weakness."

Selar seemed inclined to reply to that, but clearly she changed her mind. "We have gotten off the subject," she said, and once again seemed intensely interested in looking anywhere but at Soleta. "I have formally requested Succor. Do you understand the parameters of such a petition?"

"I believe I do," Soleta said slowly. "You are asking that I oblige myself to help you with some matter without knowing the nature of it, or what that obligation binds me to. It gives me no option to state that the request is beyond my ability to help you. Gives me no opportunity simply to refuse, for whatever reason. It is generally an application made by a fairly wretched and frightened individual who feels that she has no one on whom she can count."

"I would dispute the accuracy of the last statement . . ."

"Would you?" asked Soleta with such sudden intensity that it virtually forced Selar to look directly at her. "Would you really?"

"I . . ." Her Vulcan discipline was most impressive. Her chin ever-so-slightly outthrust, she said, "Since I am presently in the process of asking you for Succor, it would not be appropriate for me to engage in a dispute over your opinions. Believe what you wish. But I would appreciate an answer to the question."

"The answer is no."

Soleta turned on her heel and headed for the door. She was almost there when Selar halted her with a word . . .

"Please."

There was no more emotion, no more inflection in the one word than there had been in any of the words preceding it. And yet Soleta was sure that she could hear the desperation in Selar's voice. She turned back to the doctor and said flatly, the words in something of a rush, "I hereby, of my own free will, grant you Succor. In what way may I be of service."

Selar took a step forward and said, "Mind-meld with me."

"What?"

"I am concerned over my frame of mind. My concern is that my mental faculties are beginning to erode. I have been experiencing . . . feelings. Sensations. Confusions which can only be deemed inappropriate in light of my training and experience."

Slowly, Soleta sank into a chair, not taking her eyes off Selar. "You want me to mind-meld with you."

Selar paced the room, speaking in a clinically detached manner that made her feel far more comfortable than acknowledging the emotional turmoil she was straining to keep at bay. "I believe that I may be suffering the earliest stages of Bendii Syndrome, causing the disintegration of my self-control."

"If that is what you believe, then certainly there must be medical tests . . ."

But Selar shook her head. "Bendii Syndrome, at this point, would not be detectable through standard medical technologies. There are physical symptoms, yes, changes in certain waves patterns. But these are ascribable to a variety of possible ailments. It could also be Hibbs Disease, or Telemioistis . . . it could even be *Pon farr,* although that is an impossibility."

"Impossible . . . why? Timing is wrong?"

Selar suddenly felt very uncomfortable. "Yes."

"When was the last—?"

"It cannot be, believe me," Selar told her in no uncertain terms. Clearly considering the subject closed, she continued briskly, "In this situation, diagnosis via mind-meld would be the accepted and appropriate procedure to follow on Vulcan. There are doctors, psi-meds, who specialize in the technique."

"But we're not on Vulcan, and I'm not a doctor," Soleta reminded her. "This is not a situation with which I am comfortable."

"I fully understand that. However, it would not be required that you have any medical training. During the mind-meld, I will be able to use your 'outside' perspective as if it were a diagnostic tool. Were I not a doctor myself, and were I not thoroughly trained in such procedures, it would be impossible. As it stands, it is more cumbersome and inefficient than simply to have a psi-med conduct the process. But I am willing to make do."

A long moment went by, during which Soleta said nothing. Selar was no fool; Soleta's hesitation was evident. But she was not about to back off. "You have granted me Succor," she reminded her, as if the reminder were necessary. "You cannot refuse."

"True. However," and Soleta stood, squaring her shoulders. She seemed even more uncomfortable now than Selar had moments before, and she did not have the self-discipline or control to cover it as skillfully as Dr. Selar. ". . . however, I am within my rights to request that you release me from my promise. I do so now."

"I will not."

"You would force me to mind-meld with you?" Soleta made absolutely no effort to hide her surprise. "That is contrary to . . ." She couldn't even begin to articulate it. Mind-meld was a personal, private matter. To force someone to perform it upon you, or thrust your own mind into another . . . it was virtually unthinkable.

"Lieutenant, I understand your hesitation," Selar began.

"No, I do not think you do."

"We barely know one another, and you feel pressured," Selar began. "Such a mind-meld will require you to probe more deeply than one normally would. The sort of meld that is either performed between intimates, or by extremely well trained psi-meds who are capable of such private intrusions while still shielding the—"

But Soleta waved her off impatiently. "It's not about that. Not about that at all."

At this, Selar was bit surprised. "Well, then . . . perhaps you wish to explain it to me."

"I do not. Now release me from my promise."

"No."

The two women stared at each other, each unyielding in their resolve. It was Soleta who broke first. She looked away from Selar, and in a voice so soft that even Selar almost missed it, she murmured, "It is for your own good."

"My own good? Lieutenant, I need your help. That is where my 'own good' lies."

"You do not want my help."

"I believe I know what I want and—"

*"You do not **want** my **help**!"*

The outburst was so unexpected, so uncharacteristic, so un-Vulcan, that—had Selar been human—she would have gaped in undisguised astonishment. As it was she could barely contain her incredulity. Soleta looked as if someone had ripped out a piece of her soul. She was fighting to regain her composure and was only partly successful. Selar, in all her years, had never encountered a Vulcan whose emotionality was so close to the surface. All she knew was that she was beginning to feel less like a supplicant and more like a tormentor.

"I release you," she said slowly.

Soleta let out an unsteady sigh of relief. "Thank you," she said.

Clearly, now, she wanted to leave. She wanted to put as much distance between herself and Selar as she possibly could. But the reasons for her outburst, and Selar's open curiosity, were impossible to ignore. She could not pretend that it had not happened, and—despite the size of the *Excalibur*—it was, in the grand scheme of things, a small place to live when there was someone whose presence was going to make you uncomfortable. Particularly when it was someone such as the ship's CMO; not exactly the type of person one could hope never to have any interaction with.

Soleta leaned against the wall, her palms flat against it, as if requiring the support of it. She weighed all the possibilities, and came to what she realized was the only logical decision. Still, she had to protect herself. "If I tell you something relating to my medical history . . . will you treat it under the realm of doctor/patient confidentiality."

"Does it pose a threat to the health or safety of the crew of the *Excalibur?*"

The edges of Soleta's mouth, ever so slightly, turned upward. "No. No, not at all."

"Very well."

She took a deep breath. "I am . . . impure," she said. "You would not want me in your mind."

"How do you mean 'impure'? I do not understand."

"I am not . . . full Vulcan."

Selar blinked, the only outward indication of her surprise. "Your records do not indicate that." She paused, considered the information. "It is an unexpected revelation, but it is hardly cataclysmic. Your attitude, your demeanor, indicates you consider your background to be . . . shameful in some manner. Some of the greatest Vulcans in history do not have 'pure' parentage."

"I am aware of that. I am personally acquainted with Ambassador Spock."

"Personally." Selar was impressed, and made no

effort to keep it out of her voice. "May I inquire as to the circumstances?"

"We were in prison together."

Selar found this curious, to say the least, but she decided that it was probably preferable not to investigate the background of that statement. Clearly there were greater problems to be dealt with. Selar was all too aware that bedside manner was not her strong suit. And her experiences since the death of her mate, Voltak, had done nothing to soften her disposition. She knew that she had become even more distant and remote than her training would require, but she had not cared overmuch. Truthfully, since Voltak had died those two long years ago, she had not cared about anything. Nonetheless it was clear that Selar had to put aside her own concerns and deal with those of Soleta.

She placed a hand on Soleta's shoulder. Soleta looked at it as if it were an alien artifact. "Neck pinch?" she asked.

"I am endeavoring to be of comfort," Selar said formally.

"Nice try." The words had a tint of humor to them, but Soleta did not say them in an amused manner.

Slowly Selar removed her hand from Soleta's shoulder. Then she straightened her uniform jacket and said, "I do not recall your service record indicating any mixed breeding. Although I will respect the bond of doctor/patient confidentiality, falsifying your record is frowned upon. In some instances, it could even result in court-martial in the unlikely event your parentage included a hostile race such as . . ."

Her voice trailed off as she saw Soleta's expression, anticipating the word. Selar barely dared speak it. "Romulan?" she whispered.

Soleta nodded.

"You . . . lied about one of your parents being Romulan?"

But at that Soleta shook her head. Slowly she sank back down into the couch.

"My mother was Vulcan," she said softly. "I thought my father was as well. They were colonists . . . scientific researchers. Several times, in the throes of *Pon farr,* they had endeavored to conceive a child, but each time the pregnancy had resulted in miscarriage. It was a tragic circumstance for them, but they dealt with it with typical Vulcan stoicism. Besides, they had their work to keep them occupied.

"And then there came a day when my mother was on a solo exploration, my father occupied with something else. To her surprise, she came upon a downed ship, a small, one-man vessel. Deciding that there might be someone in need of rescue, she investigated. She found someone. He was a Romulan, injured from the crash. He said he was a deserter."

"A deserter?"

"So he claimed. He begged my mother not to inform anyone of his presence. His concern was that the Federation would turn him back over to the

Romulan government . . . or else put him in prison. She informed him that she could not make that promise. It would have been logical for her to lie, but my mother could not bring herself to do so. He was very angry with her, tried to stop her. She fought him and then she . . ." Soleta lowered her voice. "She learned the true nature of his background. He was not a deserter. He was an escaped criminal. A violent, amoral individual, and he . . ."

Her voice trailed off. But there was no need to finish the sentence.

Selar said nothing. She did not trust herself to be able to speak without emotion.

"When my mother returned home, she was already pregnant," said Soleta. "She contemplated having an abortion . . . and rejected it. It was not a logical decision."

"Not logical." Selar, who prized logic no less than any Vulcan, couldn't quite believe what she'd heard. "Had she aborted the pregnancy, you would not be here."

"True enough. But considering the circumstances of my conception . . . the nature of my sire . . . making certain that I was not born would have been the logical choice. But my mother and . . . the man I thought of as my father . . . they felt it . . . illogical . . . to dismiss my existence simply because of who my true father was. They were willing to take the chance that I would not be some sort of violent criminal. That their care, their training, their guidance, would be more than enough to overcome whatever unfortunate tendencies my genetic make-up might carry with it. It was a foolish gamble, but one they were willing to make. Perhaps they were not thinking clearly because of their frustrated encounters with *Pon farr*. Or perhaps they were too . . . disoriented . . . by the recent events to come to a more sensible decision. Whatever the reason, they chose to let the pregnancy proceed. This time, she did not miscarry. There is a great irony in that, I suppose."

"And you did not know the nature of your true origins?"

"No. No, I was raised in the belief that I was a full Vulcan. Neither my father nor my mother told me the truth. They saw no point in it. They felt it was information that I did not need to possess. I was, after all, my mother's daughter, and my father could not have been more devoted to me had he been my genetic parent. So you see, Doctor, there was no attempt at deception on my part. When I enrolled in Starfleet Academy, the information I provided Starfleet was correct and true, to the best of my knowledge. You should have seen me back then, Doctor. I was as pure Vulcan as anyone could ask. Cool. Unflappable. My training was thorough, my mindset absolutely ideal. I spoke in the formal English dialect favored by our people. You would never have known who my true father was. How could you? I never knew."

"What happened to him? After he . . . after the

incident with your mother, was he caught? Returned to the Romulans?"

It took an effort for Soleta to get the words out. "When my mother first returned to the colony city . . . after her violent encounter . . . my father sought out the Romulan who had abused her. But he had disappeared—repaired his ship sufficiently to escape. He eluded capture."

"And he was never found?"

"Oh . . . he was found . . ," And Soleta laughed. It was a most unusual sound, and it startled Selar profoundly. She had never heard a Vulcan laugh. "The fates, if such there be, do like their little pranks. He was caught many years after the 'incident,' as you call it. He had built up quite a reputation for himself; had a very impressive smuggling operation set up. A Starfleet vessel, the *Aldrin*, put an end to his illegal activities. And there was a junior-grade science officer aboard that vessel by the name of Soleta. She had heard about Romulans, you see, but had never had the opportunity to see one up close. She considered them to be of scientific interest, what with their being an offshoot of the Vulcan race. Her scientific curiosity drove her to walk past the brig, to observe him, to approach him and begin to ask him questions.

"And he noticed something. Something she had in her hair. A family heirloom which her mother had always worn, but had passed on to her daughter when Soleta went off to the Academy."

Selar realized immediately, saw it glinting in Soleta's hair. "The IDIC."

"Yes." Soleta tapped the IDIC pin she customarily wore in her hair. "Precisely. He was quite given to talking, the Romulan. He was rather proud of his achievements, particularly the more debased ones. I think he was, in his way, as interested in me as I was in him. I believe that he desired to see whether he could 'shock' me somehow. He proceeded to tell me the exact circumstances in which he had previously seen such a pin. The Vulcan woman who had worn one, and how he had knocked it out of her hair when he had . . . taken her forcibly. He went into intimate detail of the event. To shock me, as I said. And he did, but not in the way he had thought. For he simply believed that the recitation of the events of his brutality—his painting a vivid picture of how he had abused a Vulcan woman—would be disconcerting to me. He would have failed, for my training was too thorough. But he spoke of the world upon which he had crashed, spoke of when it happened, and there was the connection with the pin . . ." Soleta took a deep, shaky breath. "He had no idea. No idea to whom he was speaking. He thought it was simply an identical pin. A mere coincidence. And that's all it should have been, truly. I mean, the truth . . . the truth was too insane to contemplate, wasn't it. Father, all unknowing, telling his daughter the details of the rape that had led to her conception? It was . . ."

Her shoulders started to tremble, and her discipline began to crack. A single tear rolled down her cheek. Selar went to her then, tried to put a hand out, but Soleta shoved it away. Realizing the violence inherent in her move, she quickly wiped her face with the back of her hand as she said urgently, "I'm sorry, I—"

But Selar waved dismissively. "No apology necessary. Considering the circumstances . . ."

"After my encounter with my . . . with the Romulan . . . I informed Starfleet that there was an emergency of a personal nature which required my immediate attention. I had to speak to my parents in person. This was not something that could be dealt with over subspace. I returned home, returned to Vulcan, which was where my parents had relocated to in the interim. I confronted them and they . . . admitted to the true nature of my parentage. They even pointed out that they had never lied to me . . . and they had not, you know. What child, living in a normal environment, thinks to ask her father whether he is truly her father? No lie was required, for the question had never been posed. They told me that it should make no difference. That it did not diminish me, or make me less of a person than I was." Slowly she shook her head. "No difference," she repeated in clear disbelief, and then she said it again, her voice barely above a whisper, "No difference."

Selar waited. When Soleta said nothing after a time, Selar asked gently, "Did you return to Starfleet?"

"Not immediately. I could not. I felt . . .

unworthy. Despite my parents' urging, I felt I was less than the woman I was. It affected the way I conducted myself, deported myself. The way I dressed, the way I spoke . . . even to this day. Habits that I'd learned, training I had had . . . it all seemed a sham to me, somehow. Things learned by another person who was not me, but had only pretended to be me. I extended my leave of absence, and I roamed. Roamed for so long that eventually Starfleet got word to me that if I did not return, I would simply be dropped from the service. They put me in a position where I was forced to decide what to do with my life."

"Obviously you decided to return to Starfleet."

"Obviously, yes, considering that I am sitting here in a uniform. But it was not, to me, an obvious decision to make."

"What prompted you to make it, then?"

"It was my mother's dying wish."

Selar lowered her eyes. "I am . . . sorry . . . for your loss. She must have been quite young."

"All too young. Vulcans have a long life span under ideal circumstances, but that is no guarantee."

"I know that, I assure you," Selar said. Had Soleta been less self-involved, she would have detected the slight ruefulness in Selar's tone, but she did not.

Instead Soleta found herself staring at the Memory lamp which Selar had burning in her cabin. "I asked to be assigned as a teacher upon my return, and considering my lengthy departure, Starfleet saw no reason to deny my request. I was more comfortable with that situation than with the thought of continuing to wander the galaxy. However, circumstances arose so that my presence was required here."

"And you never told Starfleet of what you had learned, about your true parentage."

"No. Technically, it is withholding information. I imagine that they could make matters difficult for me, were they to learn of it. But . . . in the grand tradition of my family . . . they did not ask, and so I have had no need to lie. Convenient, is it not?"

"Very."

Soleta said nothing for a time, appearing to consider something. Finally Selar told her, "For what it is worth, Soleta . . . I do not consider you 'impure,' as the humans might say. A tortured soul, yes. But impure? No. I consider you a person of conscience and integrity. No matter what happens in the future of this vessel, I will always consider it an honor to serve with you."

"Thank you. I appreciate that. Truly, I do. And in your saying that, you've enabled me to make up my mind about something." She clapped her hands briskly and said, "Clear your mind."

"What?"

Soleta waggled her fingers and indicated that Selar should bring herself closer. "If you still desire that I probe your mind . . . that I meld with you . . . I will do so. After your sitting here patiently and listening to my life's story . . ."

"I do not wish your help out of some misplaced sense of gratitude," Selar told her.

Soleta looked at her skeptically. "Pardon me, but as I recall, a short time ago you were endeavoring to force me into aiding you through a binding blind promise, am I correct? And *now* you are concerned about the ethics involved in my helping you?"

"Matters are different now. You were," and clearly she hated to admit it, "you were correct before. I was . . . 'desperate,' if we must discuss the situation in human terms. I did not wish to depend on such relationships as friendship in order to accomplish what I felt needed to be done. But now that you have unburdened yourself . . ."

"You feel closer to me?"

"Not particularly, no. I simply feel that you have more problems than I do, and it is probably unjust to burden you with mine."

This once again prompted Soleta, in a most shocking manner, to laugh out loud. It was not something she had great experience in doing. It was a quick, awkward sound, closer to a seal bark than an actual laugh. "Your consideration is duly noted," she told her. "But I tell you honestly now, Doctor, that if you are comfortable with the situation—knowing about me what you now know—then I will assist you in your self-examination. If I say to you that it is the least I can do, I ask that you accept that in the spirit in which it's given."

Selar nodded briefly. "Very well."

She drew a chair over to the couch and sat down, facing Soleta. She cleared her thoughts, her breathing slow and steady, relaxing into the state of mind that would most facilitate the meld. Soleta did likewise, almost with a sense of relief.

Soleta did not have a tremendous amount of experience in the technique of the mind-meld, but she was certain that Selar's experience and superior training would more than make up for whatever Soleta might herself lack. Slow, methodical, unhurried, she waited until she sensed that her breathing was in complete rhythm with Selar's. Then, gently, she reached out, touching her fingers to Selar's temples.

"Our minds are merging, Selar," she said.

Their minds, their thoughts, their personas drew closer and closer to one another. The tendrils of their consciousness reached toward each other, gently probing at first . . .

. . . and then . . . contact was made . . .

. . . drawing closer still, and their thoughts began to overlap, and it was becoming hard to determine where one left off and the other began . . .

. . . and Soleta had a sense of herself, she did not lose it, it was still there, still vibrant and alive, but she had a sense of Selar as well, she was Selar, and Selar saw herself through the view of Soleta, outside her own consciousness, looking inward . . .

. . . and Selar felt uncertain and fearful, and she wasn't sure whether the insecurities rose from herself as Soleta and the knowledge of her true lineage or from herself and her concerns over her own state of mind, and she fought past it . . .

. . . and Soleta saw images flashing past her, images that were herself but not herself, images and sensations and experiences that were as real for her as they could possibly be, except none of them, absolutely none of them, had ever happened to her . . . and she began to scrutinize herself with an expertise that she had never before possessed, except it was not herself that she was scrutinizing, and yet it was, and it was with a facility that she had never had, except she did . . .

. . . and Selar felt herself slipping deeply into her own consciousness, gliding into Soleta's mind and using it as an ancient deep-sea explorer would use a bathysphere. Waves of her own thoughts and unconsciousness rippled around her as she descended further and further, moving through her psyche, and she felt waves of light pulsing around her. No, not light . . . life, her life, spread all around about her . . .

. . . and Soleta felt pain, waves of pain, and she heard voices crying out, and one of them was her own, her very own voice, and one of them was not, it was a male, it was someone she had never met in her life, and his name was Voltak, and she knew him with greater intimacy than she had ever known herself, and she could feel him moving within her . . .

. . . and Selar felt him slipping away, and Soleta

called out his name, and Selar felt his loss ripping at her, and then Soleta was suddenly yanked downward, further downward, left looking upward at Voltak in the way that a swimmer trapped beneath a frozen lake sees the face of someone above, on the ice, staring down at them . . .

. . . and Selar's mind was left naked and exposed, Soleta probing with Selar's expertise, burrowing down to the core of her psychic makeup, seeking, searching, and buffeted with wave upon wave of heat, red heat that washed over her in delicious waves of agony that she could not ignore, that swept into every pore of her skin, enveloping her, caressing her, and she moaned for the exquisite torment of it all . . .

. . . and she felt something calling her, driving her, and it was voices, not just hers, not just Soleta's and Selar's, not just Voltak's, but Vulcans, hundreds, thousands, millions of them, driving her toward the heat, toward the red waves, as if they were trying to pound her into an inferno shore, and she welcomed it, she welcomed the heat and the waves, she could not, would not turn away from it, she embraced it, wanted it, wanted it more than she had ever wanted anything, and her breath was coming in short gasps, their minds slamming together . . .

My God . . .

The separation was violent. Soleta yanked away from her, and Selar tumbled backward, the chair overturning and spilling her onto her back. Soleta fell over, rolled off the couch and onto the floor. She lay there panting, gasping, her fingers still spasming as sensations shook her body. Sweat was dripping off her forehead, spattering onto the floor. With supreme effort she managed to look over at Selar, who didn't appear to be in much better shape. Selar was lying on her back, her arms outstretched, sucking in air gratefully, as if she had forgotten to breathe for however long they had been joined. It clearly took tremendous effort but slowly Selar turned her head and managed to look at Soleta. Soleta, for her part, felt embarrassed, like a voyeur, even though it had been Selar who had asked for the probe.

Selar was trying to mouth a word. Soleta propped herself up on one elbow and angled herself closer to Selar, just close enough to hear her say it:

"Impossible" was the low whisper. Selar had now actually managed to muster enough strength to shake her head, and again she murmured, "Impossible."

"Apparently . . . not." Soleta was surprised, even impressed, with the calm in her voice. Ever since learning the truth of her background, stoicism had not been something that she had always been able to maintain. Here, though, she was clearly capable of rising to the occasion. "Apparently it's not impossible at all."

"But it was . . . it was barely two years ago . . . I . . . I went through it . . . not time . . . not for years, it is not time . . ."

"Perhaps it's because of the way that it ended the first time," Soleta said reasonably. "The urge was never truly satisfied, but because you were mind-melded at the time . . . it sent you into a sort of psychic shock . . . numbed you . . . but it's finally worn off . . ."

"You . . . you do not know . . . what you are saying . . ." Selar's face had gone dead white.

"Maybe not," agreed Soleta. "Maybe I don't know what I'm saying at all. Maybe I'm completely crazy . . . except I know what I saw, Selar. I know what I felt and experienced. Whether you like it or not, whether you want to admit it or not . . . what you're going through right now is the first stages of *Pon farr.* Your bad experience the first time threw your system off, but now the mating frenzy is back with a vengeance. And I have absolutely no idea what you're going to do about it."

And Selar had the sick feeling that, somewhere in the ship, Burgoyne was sniffing the air and grinning. And she wasn't far wrong.

VII.

THROUGH THE CORRIDORS of the *Kayven Ryin*, Si Cwan moved with the utmost care, flexing his arm to work out the kinks in his shoulder.

He was alone.

He had given Zak Kebron the slip, for Kebron had quickly made it clear he had no intention of letting Cwan handle matters the way he wanted to. The idea of not using any of the hand weapons, for starters, was intolerable to Kebron. In his arrogance—at least, arrogance the way Si Cwan saw it—Kebron felt that he himself did not have to depend on weapons. But he was of the forceful opinion that if Si Cwan had the opportunity to use a weapon on Zoran, he should take it. That nothing was going to be accomplished by treating the situation as a grudge match.

But this had gone far beyond grudges. Si Cwan

knew, beyond any question, that he was going to kill
Zoran. He simply had to. Honor would not allow
anything less. And he had to do it with his bare
hands. This was not a question of honor allowing
anything less, but rather his simple determination to
make Zoran's punishment as painful as possible.

So Si Cwan had, moving quickly, left the Brikar
behind. He'd been subtle about it; give him some
credit. He'd darted down a corridor at a faster clip
than the Brikar could maintain, and then run off
down a connector, slid through a maintenance tube,
and next thing he knew, he was on his own. And if he
should live long enough to be in a position where he
need make excuses, he could always simply claim
that they had become accidentally separated from
one another. Accidents, after all, did happen.

He heard a noise.

It was definitely not Zak Kebron. He already knew
that rock-steady footfall. No, it was quick, extremely
light-footed. He would almost have thought it was
the movement of a small animal, so fast and nearly
insubstantial was it. But Si Cwan wasn't fooled, not
for a moment.

He crouched down and moved like a giant spider,
arms and legs operating in perfect synchronization.
He presented as minimal a target as possible, should
it come to that.

He moved past one room, the door to which was
closed, and from within he thought he heard something. A quick footfall, or perhaps something on a
table within that was slightly jolted and sent skid-

ding. Something. He paused outside the door, crouching to one side, trying to determine whether or not he should burst into the room. It could very well be that someone was waiting for him to do precisely that, and had a vicious weapon aimed squarely at the door.

Or perhaps they had anticipated that he would think entry through the door was a trap . . . and were instead aimed at the ceiling, or at a vent, hoping that he would make his entry that way.

He still had the plasma blaster slung across his shoulders, and practicality began to rear its ugly head. He still had every reason to want to throttle Zoran . . . but by the same token, he had a few more reasons to want to continue to live.

Well . . . perhaps using the plasma blaster wouldn't be such a crime after all, as long as the killing blow was struck by hand. That was, after all, the important thing.

He unslung the blaster, aimed it squarely at the door, and fired. At such close range, the plasma blast plowed through the door like acid through paper, and Si Cwan leaped headlong through the door, shoulder rolled and came up to face . . .

. . . nothing.

He was inside a laboratory, and there was no evidence of anyone else there. There was a beaker rolling across a table. Other than that, nothing.

He muttered a curse as he slung the plasma blaster over his back. The noise of the plasma blaster would undoubtedly attract Zoran or his compatriots there.

Or else Kebron himself, which would leave Si Cwan with explaining to do and an undesired ally at his back. Si Cwan felt that if there was one thing he did not need, it was someone watching out for him.

He thought that up until the moment that the ceiling crashed in on him.

It caught him completely by surprise as an overhead grating slammed down onto him, driving him to his knees. A split second later, Zoran dropped down from his hiding place overhead inside one of the engineering service ducts, and landed squarely on Si Cwan's back.

He drove a vicious blow to the base of Si Cwan's neck, to the hard cluster of muscles situated there, and by all rights it should have paralyzed Si Cwan from the neck down for approximately five minutes. In the short term, it did the job. Si Cwan thudded to the ground, unable to feel anything in the rest of his body. The fall spilled Zoran to the floor as well, but Zoran rolled away and came quickly to his feet. Si Cwan struggled furiously, trying to regain command over his movements, as a sneering Zoran approached him.

"Too easy. Much too easy," he said.

The humans had a phrase for it: mind over matter. The mind belonged to Cwan, and the matter was—in this instance—his own body. He refused to acknowledge the physical reality that he was helpless. He would not allow himself to die helplessly in a paralyzed condition. It simply could not, would not be done. His brain sent commands to the rest of his body to respond, sending synapses roaring through him like photon torpedoes.

Against all odds, against anything that Zoran would have deemed possible, Si Cwan's legs slammed upward. They did not do so with all the force that they usually possessed. But it was sufficient as his legs scissored around Zoran's at the knees. Before Zoran could move, Si Cwan forced himself to twist at the waist. He felt sluggish, torpid, but slow for Si Cwan was still lightning for most anyone else. The move was enough to collapse Zoran's leg, and Zoran went down to find himself on the floor, face-to-face with the enraged Si Cwan.

Si Cwan rolled over, half leaping and half lunging toward Zoran. He landed squarely on his opponent, grabbed him firmly by the ears, yanked upward and then down, slamming Zoran's head onto the grated floor. Zoran's head rang from the impact, and with a roar and an effort fueled by the explosion of pain behind his eyes, Zoran shoved Si Cwan off himself. Si Cwan rolled over toward a table, saw an opportunity, and quickly upended the table, sending it tumbling toward Zoran. Zoran barely managed to scramble out of the way, and by the time he was on his feet, so was Si Cwan.

They stood there for a moment, catching their respective breaths, their chests heaving, their hatred almost palpable.

"It's been ages, Si Cwan," snarled Zoran.

"Where are the other two? Rojam and Juif, they must be nearby."

"You don't think I'd give away our strategic position, do you?" In point of fact, they were nowhere nearby. The confrontation was strictly between Zoran and Si Cwan, which was how Zoran had wanted it.

Yet Si Cwan smiled with thinly veiled contempt and said, "Did you embark on this stupidity on your own? Or, even better . . . did they accompany you on this endeavor and then take the opportunity to abandon you? Is that it? Have your cheerfully domineering ways managed to grate on them after all these years? That would not surprise me. No, not in the least."

Rallying himself, Zoran said, "Tell me, Si Cwan, what it is like knowing that you are a complete and total failure?"

Si Cwan did not even deign to answer the question. He merely tossed a disdainful look at him.

"I see you have a weapon on your back," continued Zoran. "And yet you would not use it."

"I've known you too long, Zoran. I knew that you would desire to settle this hand-to-hand, between the two of us. In many ways, you're sadly predictable."

"In many ways, so are you. The difference between us is, I make use of that predictability . . . and you don't."

And Zoran snapped his arm forward in what seemed an oddly casual gesture, as if he were endeavoring to shake hands.

A short blade hurtled out from his sleeve, thudding deeply into Si Cwan's already injured upper shoulder. Si Cwan let out an angry roar and tried to pull it out, but the tip was barbed and it wasn't going to be easy to remove. Nor was Zoran giving him the time, for Zoran vaulted the distance between the two of them, grabbed the blade by the handle, and twisted it. Pain screamed through Si Cwan, and he howled in fury.

"Enjoying your vengeance, Si Cwan?" asked Zoran as he wrenched the dagger around in place. Blood fountained from the gaping wound in Si Cwan.

But in order to handle the dagger, Zoran had had to get close in to Si Cwan, giving him opportunity to strike back. The base of Si Cwan's hand slammed into the bridge of Zoran's nose, and the crack—like a ricochet—sounded in the room. The world hazed red to Zoran, and suddenly he felt Si Cwan's hands at his throat. Cwan's thumbs dug in and upward, seeking out the choke hold, cutting off Zoran's air.

"I don't care what happens to me," Si Cwan said hoarsely, his voice a growl, "and I don't care how I die, as long as you die first."

Zoran drove a knee up into Si Cwan's gut. Si Cwan grunted, ignoring the pain, beyond its ability to influence him. He was focused on one goal: choking the life from Zoran. His hands were locked securely on, all his strength dedicated to the effort. The rest of the world seemed to evaporate around him. There was just Zoran, and him, and the feel of Zoran's pulse beneath his fingers which Si Cwan was determined to extinguish.

He started to force Zoran down, down to his knees, and Zoran cried out in pain and fear. And in desperation, Zoran managed to slam his head forward against the hilt of the dagger, driving it in even deeper.

Si Cwan had no choice. The knife struck a muscle which, as a reflex, caused Si Cwan's hands to flex open just for a moment. It was all Zoran needed as he tore himself away, literally throwing his body the distance of the lab. He crashed to the floor just inside the door.

Dark liquid covered the entire front of Si Cwan's tunic, but he didn't care. Like an unswerving juggernaut, he lurched toward Zoran, fingers still opening and closing spasmodically as if he still had Zoran's throat between them. As if he was positive that it would only be a matter of moments before he once again had Zoran's life in his hands.

There was much that Zoran had fancied about Si Cwan, for it had been several years since he had actually set eyes on him. There was much that he had managed to convince himself of. Once upon a time, he had spent days hunting by Si Cwan's side. He had wrestled with him, sparred with him, confided in him, given Si Cwan his confidence and received it in return. For the purpose of rationalizing the split that had occurred between them, Zoran had indulged in that habit which most sentient beings engaged in when separating from old friends: demonizing. Zoran had told so many people that Si Cwan was a fake, a fraud, a lazy bastard who was more lucky than skilled, and of whom everyone had been afraid because of his station in life, that Zoran had more or less convinced himself of that as well.

So it was very disturbing for Zoran to find himself in combat with Si Cwan now and come to the stark realization that his memory had played tricks on him. He had convinced himself that, face-to-face, hand-to-hand, he could easily handle Si Cwan.

Now he realized that, at the very least, he could handle Si Cwan but with extreme difficulty. Extreme difficulty meant that a good deal of time was going to be occupied accomplishing it. And time was something he did not have in abundance.

He tapped the comm-link unit on his wrist even as he backpedaled into the corridor. "All right, enough! Beam me out!"

That was when Zoran felt the ground starting to tremble beneath him. He glanced off to his right and saw what appeared to be a walking landmass advancing on him. Zak Kebron charged forward, arms pumping.

Then Zoran heard a defiant war cry and his attention was yanked back to Si Cwan. Cwan had actually ripped the barbed dagger from his shoulder, which should have been impossible. At the very least, any normal person would have collapsed in agony by that point. But if there was any doubt in Zoran's mind that Si Cwan was far from normal, it would certainly have been settled by now.

The dagger was dripping with Si Cwan's blood. He

could not have cared less. He tossed it aside, sending it clattering across the floor leaving a trail of red behind him. And then he lurched forward toward Zoran.

One hand was outstretched, his palm covered with thick, dark fluids; his own.

He didn't care.

He had a weapon still strapped to his back.

He didn't care.

He was injured, wounded, every muscle in his body aching, and weak from blood loss. And Si Cwan didn't care.

The only thing he cared about was getting his hands on Zoran. Which, ultimately, he was unable to do.

A sound filled the immediate area. Although it was of a different timbre than the noise produced by a regulation Starfleet transporter, nonetheless it was easily identifiable as a matter transporter sound.

"No!" howled Si Cwan in outrage, and in desperation he leaped at Zoran. His hope was that if he managed to leap into range of the transport effect in time, he would be brought along to wherever it was that Zoran was heading. But he was too late. Zoran's form became just insubstantial enough for Si Cwan to fall right through it. He hit the metal grating of the floor as Zoran—along with Si Cwan's chances for revenge—disappeared.

"Get back here, you bastard!" shouted Si Cwan, slamming his fists on the floor in frustration.

"I doubt he'll hear you," observed Kebron, who had chugged to a halt just short of running Si Cwan over.

Then the comm unit that Si Cwan had taken off of the fallen Thallonian beeped. There was no question in his mind who it was who was endeavoring to get in touch with him. He activated it and said angrily, "I call you coward, Zoran!"

"I call you dead, Si Cwan," Zoran replied with just a touch of regret. "But if you wish to discuss it further, I suggest you adjourn to a location two decks below you, aft section." And he clicked off.

Without hesitation, Si Cwan pivoted and started off in the direction that Zoran had indicated, but he was brought to an abrupt halt by Kebron, who had gotten a firm grip on his arm. "No you don't. Not again."

"I'm not going to let him get away!"

"You already did. If you mean you won't let him get away *again,* that's up for debate."

"Kebron, let go of me!" he said with angry imperiousness. And then, in a tone that was a bit more pleading, he added, "Please."

"We go together. On your honor. Say it."

Si Cwan gritted his teeth and nodded reluctantly. "Together. But you will not interfere in the outcome. On your honor. Say it. Say you will do nothing to interfere in the outcome of the battle between Zoran and myself."

"If you insist. On my honor, I will not interfere in the outcome of the battle."

"Very well. Let's go." And he charged off, but slowly enough that Kebron could keep up.

Zoran stared out at the depths of space which beckoned to them. Rojam and Juif stood on either side of him, fidgeting nervously, staring at the darkened navigation console of their escape vessel. It was not a particularly large ship; indeed, joined as it was to the airlock of the *Kayven Ryin,* it had actually avoided the *Marquand* detecting it. It had room enough for three people, and also a single transport pad, which Rojam had used to get Zoran off the science vessel to which they were still attached.

"Zoran, get us out of here," Juif said urgently.

It was difficult to tell whether Zoran had actually heard him. He simply sat there, jaw set, anger flickering in his eyes.

Rojam crouched down and said sharply, "Zoran . . . I wish, for your sake, you had defeated him in the manner you desired. But we had a deal. We gave you your ten minutes. The bomb is set. Further delay risks all our lives."

In a faintly mocking tone, Juif added, "It is the province of Si Cwan and his ilk to make promises that they do not keep."

Slowly Zoran turned to them, appearing to notice them for the first time since he'd been beamed aboard the escape vessel. "I am curious," he said. "If I had not rigged this vessel so that its flight systems would only respond to my voice commands . . . would you have left me on the ship? Left me behind to die with Si Cwan? Or did you only stick to our plan because you needed me in order to escape?"

"Don't be ridiculous," Rojam said flatly, and Juif echoed the sentiment.

Zoran looked into their eyes, tried to see the true feelings there. "You are afraid," he said after a moment.

"Of course we're afraid!" Juif told him in mounting exasperation. "We're attached to a vessel that's going to be space dust in a few minutes, and you're quizzing us over our devotion as your friends! Cut us loose from here and let's be done with it! We can discuss this all you want later, but if we don't break off now, there's not going to be a later!"

Zoran stared at them for a moment that seemed to stretch out into forever, and then he said, "Nav computer, voice ID, Zoran Si Verdin."

"Voice ID confirmed," the computer replied indifferently.

"Nav systems on line. Detach vessel from airlock. Set heading to 183 on the Y-axis. Activate."

"Activating."

There was a slight jostling, the sound of huge metal clamps releasing, and a moment later they were free of their moorings. The escape vessel dropped away from the doomed science vessel *Kayven Ryin* and arced away into the blackness of space.

And they didn't even notice that, far in the distance, something was starting to ripple into existence . . .

* * *

Si Cwan crept forward, and then was very un-nerved as Zak Kebron strode by, making no attempt at subtlety. "Kebron!" he hissed angrily. "Zoran is just ahead! A little stealth would be appreciated!"

Kebron looked at him blandly. "I'm Brikar," he informed him. "I don't do 'stealth.'"

Si Cwan rolled his eyes.

"Besides," continued Kebron, marching ahead, floor rattling beneath him, "I suspect that the question will be moot. I don't think Zoran is there."

"What?"

"It would be foolish to blithely give away a position or the advantage of surprise in that manner."

"You don't know Zoran as I do," said Si Cwan, moving just behind Kebron.

"No, I do not. As a result, I assess him calmly and coldly, rather than letting my opinion be clouded by hatred. I tell you that such a move on his part would be sheer foolishness, and nothing that you've told me about him indicates that level of stupidity."

"What do you think to expect, then?"

"A trap."

Si Cwan blew air impatiently out between his teeth. "I can handle any trap of Zoran's."

They rounded a corner and then Kebron came to such an abrupt halt that Si Cwan banged into his back, crunching his face into Kebron's spine. He stepped back, rubbing his nose, about to complain angrily . . . and then he saw it.

It was large and cylindrical, with moorings that

had fused it to the floor, ceiling, and walls so that it was impossible to move. It beeped imperturbably, and it was counting down.

Si Cwan's face darkened as Kebron turned to face him. "All right, Cwan. All yours. Handle it."

Si Cwan approached it tentatively. There was a small display on the face of it, counting down. "I think it's a bomb," he said.

"Yes. A superheated thermite bomb, if I'm not mistaken. From the readings and the power escalation, I'd say it's going to detonate within two minutes. If I had to guess, I'd surmise that Zoran is long gone, and has left us to the bomb's nonexistent mercies."

Trying to fight down desperation, Si Cwan's fingers explored the outer casing. It was seamless. "Kebron, I'm no munitions expert. You have to disarm it."

"I have sworn I would not interfere in the outcome of the battle. The bomb was obviously left by Zoran; it's part of the battle. For me to take any action would be in violation of my oath. It would be dishonorable. I'm afraid I can't do that."

Si Cwan looked at him with undisguised incredulity. "Is this some Brikar idea of a joke?"

"I'm quite serious." He paused. "You could, of course, release me from my vow . . ."

"I release you! *I release you!*"

The moment he heard that, Kebron crossed quickly to the bomb and began to look it over. Putting his strength into it, he attempted to twist open the casing. When it resisted his efforts, he pulled experimentally at the moorings, and then with greater force. The metal bars held firm. He paused, contemplated the situation a moment, and then turned to Si Cwan and put a large hand on Cwan's shoulder. "May you have the eyes of the gods upon you, and success and glory in all future endeavors."

"Don't just yammer at me! *Do* something!"

"I *am* doing something," he said unflappably. "I'm wishing you well in the afterlife. Aside from that, my options are somewhat limited."

"Disarm the bomb!"

"With two hours to work on it and a Starfleet bomb squad backing me up, that might be an option. As it is . . ."

"You have a phaser. Shoot it! Disintegrate it!"

"Any attempt to do so will set it off. Furthermore, do you see this indicator?" and he pointed to one panel. "It's a motion sensor. Any attempt to move the bomb will also set it off."

Si Cwan was already in motion. "Let's go."

"Where?" asked Kebron curiously.

"To the far end of the ship!"

"Cwan, when this thing goes off in under a minute now, *every* part of the ship is going to be the far end. It's going to be scattered all over the system."

In helpless frustration, Si Cwan stared at the bomb and came to the same realization that Kebron had come to the moment he'd seen it.

There was a long silence, and then Si Cwan turned

to Kebron and said, "I want you to understand: I am not afraid of death. In some ways, it's almost a blessing. But it angers me that I die while Zoran gets away. It angers me very much."

"Life is loose ends."

Si Cwan nodded, watching the bomb tick down, and then he patted Kebron on the shoulder. "You are a fine warrior, Kebron. I regret that we did not have more time to work out our differences. At least . . . at least I go to be with my sister, as you go to be with your parents."

"My parents." Kebron looked at him blankly.

"Yes. Your parents. Killed on the mining colony by Orion . . . pirates . . ."

"Oh, that," and Kebron's massive shoulders moved in something akin to a shrug. "It seemed like a convenient thing to tell you at the time. Actually, my parents live on Brikar. My mother is a politician, my father a salesman of motivational programs. They're alive and well. Thank you for your concern, though."

Si Cwan stared at him. "You made it up?"

"Of course I did. I wanted you to feel we had something in common so that you'd listen to me rather than run about like an idiot. So much for *that* plan."

The bomb ticked down to zero.

"I hate you," said Si Cwan.

And the ship blew up.

LAHEERA

VIII.

Calhoun was on his way up to the bridge, anxious to speak with Shelby and Lefler, who had just returned from the surface of Nelkar. In heading to the turbolift, however, he met Selar in the corridor. "Doctor," he greeted her, his voice carefully neutral.

"Captain," she replied, inclining her head in return and continuing on her way.

Unable to resist, he turned and said, "Dr. Selar . . . is everything all right?"

She stopped and faced him, her arms folded across her chest. "That is a broad question, sir. Could you be more specific?"

"I could. Are you going to force me to be?"

She simply stood there, staring at him with feigned disinterest.

"All right." He took a step forward. "I—"

Then his comm badge beeped, and he tapped it. "Calhoun here."

"Captain, we're receiving a communication from the Nelkarites," came Shelby's voice.

"On my way," he said. "Doctor . . . we'll continue this later."

"I look forward to it, sir," she told him, and it was only after Calhoun had walked off that she came to the startled realization that she'd just told her first lie.

Calhoun walked out onto the bridge, noting that Soleta was back at her science station, and reasoning that it would be pointless to pump her for information regarding Selar. From the tactical station, Boyajian said, "On screen, sir?"

"Not yet. Shelby, Lefler . . . report, please." He sat in the command chair and steepled his fingers.

"The facilities that we were shown for the refugees, although hardly luxurious, are far from spartan," Shelby informed him. "The Nelkarites seem genuinely interested in providing aid, and accepting the refugees into their society."

"And the refugees desire to remain there?"

"They have made that quite clear. I even suggested that they return to the *Excalibur* for a final debriefing; instead they voted amongst themselves, and it was unanimously requested that their possessions be sent down to Nelkar. They wish to stay. They seem happy there."

"I'm overjoyed," Calhoun said with what seemed a significant lack of enthusiasm. "Lefler?"

"Their society is not terribly advanced by our standards. They seem . . . 'lazy' doesn't seem the right word. 'Unmotivated,' perhaps. They have no major scientific research programs. They merely acquire things from other races and use those things to advance themselves. They sort of 'piggyback' on the accomplishments of others."

"All right. Recommendations?"

"There doesn't seem to be much to offer in that department, Captain," Shelby said. "The refugees have made their desires clear. They wish to stay on Nelkar. We cannot interfere in their stated wishes, nor should we. It would be contrary to the Prime Directive. More than that . . . it would border on the tyrannical."

Calhoun looked at her with mild surprise. "Commander . . . I may be many things. But 'tyrant' is hardly among them."

"I'm very aware of that, sir," she said reasonably. "That's why I'm afraid there really isn't much choice."

He drummed his fingers on the armrest for a moment. "It certainly appears that way. All right, Boyajian . . . put them on screen."

A moment later, an opulent room appeared on the monitor. There was Captain Hufmin, swathed in fine blue robes. There was a smile plastered on his face, and considering the drink in his hand and the manner in which he was swaying, the smile wasn't the only thing that was plastered. Next to him was Laheera, and the somewhat inebriated Hufmin was no longer making any attempt to hide his leering appraisal of her.

"Hello, Captain Calhoun," Laheera said, in that musical voice of hers.

"Greetings," Calhoun replied evenly. "From what my first officer tells me, you've made quite an impression on our passengers. And, if I might note, on Captain Hufmin as well."

"Yes, so it would appear," she commented. "And now we have matters to discuss, Captain."

"I'm told there isn't much to discuss, actually," Calhoun said with a subtle glance at Shelby. "We'll be beaming down our passengers' belongings, and be on our way. It is my hope that they'll be happy in their new home."

"I'm certain they will be, Captain Calhoun . . . once you cooperate."

Although her voice never lost its pleasant inflection, there was an undertone to the words that was not lost on anyone on the bridge. It was, however, lost on Hufmin, who was leaning against Laheera and grinning in a lopsided fashion.

"Cooperate?" Calhoun said slowly.

"Yes. You see, Captain, you have very advanced technology. Computer systems, weapons systems, warp drive capabilities that far exceed—"

"Not to be rude, Laheera, but . . . you might as well stop right there. Don't think that we're not grateful that you've opened your home and hearts to the refugees. But I simply cannot turn over technology to you." He rose from his chair and walked slowly to the monitor, sounding as reasonable as he could. "There are rules we live by, laws we follow, just as I'm sure you have your own laws. Your society is at a certain level, and it wouldn't be right or proper for us to aid you in jumping to the next. You have to reach that point yourselves."

"We have selflessly extended aid," Laheera said with a slight pout that made her look, frankly, just adorable. "Can't you do the same for us? It makes you seem a bit selfish."

"It sure does!" Hufmin agreed. Then again, in his condition and with the nearness of Laheera adding to his intoxication, he would have agreed that the sun was actually made of steamed cabbage.

"It does make us seem that way," Calhoun acknowledged. "But believe me, Laheera, it's for the best."

"I'm afraid I can't agree with that," said Laheera.

"That's right, Captain," Hufmin echoed, "she can't agree with th—"

It happened so quickly that Lefler, who happened to be blinking at that exact moment, didn't see it. But the others on the bridge did.

The knife was in Laheera's hand, and she grabbed the grinning Hufmin by the hair with her other hand, snapping his head backward. The most eerie thing was that her smile never wavered as she expertly yanked the knife across Hufmin's throat. Blood poured out and down, his blue robes turning deep crimson. Some of it spattered on Laheera's face, red speckling the gold. She didn't appear to notice or care. Hufmin did not even realize he'd been murdered. He reached up in a vague manner for the gash and he was grinning insipidly, probably feeling the warmth as it gushed all over him, and then he sank down and out of sight.

Shelby, horrified, looked to Calhoun.

His face looked dead. There was no expression at all—not anger, not revulsion—nothing. But then she saw it, saw it in his purple eyes: a deep, burning, savage fury that was barely contained.

In an almost absentminded fashion, Laheera reached down to wipe the blood off the blade. It was obvious, even though they couldn't see it, that she had cleaned it on the fallen Hufmin. "Now," Laheera said conversationally, "I did that in order to show you that we will not hesitate to do whatever is necessary to get what we want. We will kill the refugees. All of them. Men, women, children . . . makes no difference. We shall begin killing them shortly and continue to do so until you supply us with the technology we need. We will give you one hour to think about it and get back in touch with you at the end of that ti—"

"No."

The word sounded like a death knell. Calhoun had said it with no hesitation, no remorse, and no sense of pity whatsoever.

Laheera tilted her head slightly, like a dog trying

to hear a high-pitched noise. "You mean you've already decided to cooperate with us?"

"No," said Calhoun. "I mean no, there will be no deals. No, there will not be a discussion. And no, you needn't wait. Kill them."

Lefler gasped upon hearing this. Soleta kept her composure, but McHenry paled, and even Shelby appeared shaken. Calhoun looked at her and she mouthed the word, *Negotiate*.

Laheera didn't quite seem to believe she'd heard or understood Calhoun correctly. "Captain . . . perhaps you don't appreciate the severity of the situation . . ."

"My first officer," Calhoun cut in, "appears to be of the opinion that I should negotiate."

"She is wise."

Calhoun walked up to the main screen, his back straight, his eyes now cold. "Laheera . . . the refugees made their own decision. I gave them advice. They ignored it. Whatever situation they're in now is of their own making. I have no sympathy for them that you can play upon. No guilt. No compunction about letting them die. They made their free choice, and they die as free beings. Nor do I wish to negotiate with terrorists. There is no point to it."

"My understanding, Captain, from what the late Captain Hufmin told me, is that you were something of a terrorist yourself once," Laheera said. It was frightening how the singsong tone of voice never wavered. "Who are you, then, to judge me?"

There was dead silence on the bridge for a long moment.

And when Calhoun spoke, there was something terrifying in his voice. No one on the bridge had ever heard anything like it. It was as if an approaching natural disaster, like a tornado or an ion storm, had been given voice to declare the dreadful damage it was about to inflict.

"You desire negotiation, Laheera? That I will not do. I don't negotiate. That is an immutable law of my universe. Another immutable law, however, is one of physics: that for every action, there is an equal and opposite reaction. Kill the refugees, Laheera. Kill them all. I don't care. I've seen too much death to let it be used as a club against me. But when you're done killing them, be aware that you've killed yourselves. Because I will order this ship to open fire on your capital city and blow you all to hell. Who am I to judge you, Laheera? I am someone who knows what it's like to deal with someone like me. Calhoun out."

TO BE CONTINUED

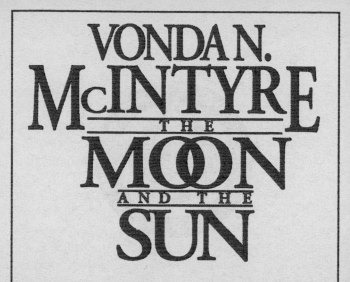

VONDA N. McINTYRE
THE MOON AND THE SUN

From the gifted imagination of the *New York Times* bestselling author comes a breathtaking work of epic dimensions. Part adventure story, part legend, and part gothic novel, this is a tale of alternate history so richly evocative it defies definition.

"Luminous."
—Ursula K. Le Guin

**Coming in Hardcover mid-August 1997
From Pocket Books**

POCKET
BOOKS

COMING IN AUGUST!

Day of Honor
Book One:

ANCIENT BLOOD
by
Diane Carey

Turn the page for an excerpt from Book One of
Star Trek: Day of Honor

And a Special
Offer from Pocket Books

Anger bled into Worf's heart as the eyes of the Klingon guards, the Rogues, fixed upon him and he felt their animosity.

The woman, Odette Khanty, nodded to her Klingon vanguard to keep moving forward in spite of Worf, who was blocking their path.

Klingons. Klingons in service to a human. A human criminal.

Klingons who had simply rejected anything Klingons are supposed to think about right and wrong, not here because of a sense of honorable conquest, duty, family loyalty, or anything else Klingons might be motivated by. These had just thrown all that away, cast off centuries of attachment to Klingon culture. These Klingons were destructively seeking personal power, rather than acting in a way that would hold society, even Klingon society, together. Profit and gain could be pursued in a manner that strengthened culture, but these Klingons wanted to go around those rules and achieve their ends through the basest of brutality and opportunism.

Scum. Nothing. He was looking at empty hoods. Empty!

"Ugulan." Mrs. Khanty's voice sounded in the quiet square as she spoke to the sergeant of her guard. "The Klingon."

"Yes, Mrs. Khanty." As if he didn't notice that he himself was Klingon and so were all his men, Ugulan motioned for the guards to halt, but they remained in formation around her.

Then Ugulan himself stepped forward, his face deeply shaded by the purple hood. He moved through the empty tables to the one where Worf sat defiantly. With his hood and the dagger at his belt, Ugulan was effectively threatening.

"You will stand aside for Mrs. Odette Khanty to pass through," he said.

Grant looked at Worf, but said nothing.

Worf sipped his drink, took a long, considered swallow, then said, "I will not be moved."

"All citizens must stand aside when a public official comes through," Ugulan insisted. His tone implied this would be the last polite suggestion.

Worf looked up at him. "I am not a citizen. Therefore I do not move."

Ugulan's dagger swung upward as if to be its own exclamation point, and was on the downward arch when Worf came to life. Ah! At last! His move was extremely simple and not particularly inspired, a basic block of Ugulan's arm, but Worf imagined he had Ugulan nearly figured out already and could afford to not be creative.

He was right. Thrown off, Ugulan clattered into a stand of empty iron chairs. The chairs went over, clanging like gongs against the brickwork street, and Ugulan went down among them. By the time he had scrambled to one knee, Worf was squared off between Ugulan and Grant, standing ground like a living portcullis.

One of the other Rogues clasped Mrs. Khanty's arm to draw her away from the developing trouble, but she resisted.

Not waiting for Ugulan to get entirely to his feet, Worf freely charged the guard, driving him into a parqueted wall and knocking a stenciled sign from its hook. Ugulan's hood fell from his head, revealing his spinelike brown ridge and showing clearly that he too was a Klingon, as if there had been a bit of doubt.

Worf had clung to that silly doubt, but now his rage drove down his illogic.

Angry now, Ugulan reached into his jacket and drew his government phaser.

Worf didn't back off. "So," he said, "the Rogue Force of Sindikash uses women's weapons."

Evidently one of the universe's classic simpletons, Ugulan allowed himself to be goaded. He thrust to his feet and accommodated his opponent by holstering the phaser and bringing the dagger forward again.

Guarding Mrs. Khanty, the other Rogues were furious too. Any who had his phaser out now put it away.

"You're so predictable, boys," the woman commented.

"Let us!" Genzsha demanded.

Would they make no move without her permission? Worf asked himself.

"Go," she said.

Two of the Rogues stayed with her, but the forward four rushed to Ugulan's side and all squared off against Worf.

The big contenders circled slowly against the square's buildings. By appearance, Klingons fit well among the medieval-dye colors of Sindikash— earthy, moody, deep and stirring colors that gave an impression of permanent autumn, flickering with gilded designs crafted from the planet's mica- like ores. Even the brickwork imitated the woven texture of Persian-style carpets the colony was famous for.

It also made a mean surface to knock against. Hitting a wall on Sindikash was entirely different from hitting a wall anywhere else. The walls here had exposed dentils of brick, and the newcomer made good use of that. Careful not to let Ugulan get a grip on him, Worf shoved him and two other Rogues into the same wall so hard that the impact set a stained glass window rattling. They all came up again, but the ragged brickwork left them bruised and gashed. If only all planets cooperated so well.

Holographers who had been following Mrs. Khanty and the Rogues sprang forward now and began recording the moment. Some even dared skirt the onlookers or dodge through the grappling Klingons so they could get images of Mrs. Khanty standing here, watching calmly.

A silk wall covering shivered as Worf blew past, with two Rogues in his grip. The cafe became a blur of kicks, spins, elbows, and grunts. Stacks of etched clay urns dissolved and skittered across the brick, matched instantly by the audible crack of a limb. Worf almost stopped to make sure the limb wasn't his—then decided a broken arm would only make him angrier and that might help.

An instant later, though, one of the Rogues went down groaning. Genzsha moved forward to drag his fallen comrade from the arena, but did not join the fight himself.

Worf decided he would have to do without a broken arm, and therefore crammed his elbow into the face of a second Rogue and knocked him silly. Two down.

He knew he might be giving himself away. If they paid any attention, they would certainly see his Starfleet training in his movements. Worf fought using not just the systematic moves of a schooled Klingon but uneven elements of surprise, attack, and feint, and he never let his timing or style be mapped. Just when he was expected to block a punch, Worf would let it through but dodge it, ripping every tendon in his attacker's arm. Though two remaining Rogues were still fighting, they were also dizzy and grunting.

Driven by the personal insult these men were to him, Worf took on both at once, not allowing them to divide the attack, as they attempted. He took a vicious blow from one, but instead of swinging back he reached out to the other and dragged them together before him.

Then, with physical control that surprised even himself, Worf lowered his arms and stood very still. His shoulders went slack. His stance changed. He stopped fighting.

Since he stopped, the two remaining Rogues could no longer be justified in attacking him again. Like wolves twitching around a stag who refused to run, they blinked, gaped, shifted, and glanced back at Mrs. Khanty, not knowing what to do. Boiling with frustration, Ugulan shouted a command in Klingon, and the Rogues grappled the newcomer.

Their eyes rolled with contempt, for he had humiliated them by stopping. Clearly, they knew, Worf hadn't had to let himself be captured.

Worf's plan was a success.

Look for STAR TREK Fiction from Pocket Books

Star Trek®: The Original Series

Star Trek: The Next Generation®

Star Trek: Deep Space Nine®